TAMBURLAINE MUST DIE

The Cutting Room

TAMBURLAINE
MUST DIE

Louise Welsh

CANONGATE

Edinburgh · New York · Melbourne

First published in Great Britain in 2004 by
Canongate Books Ltd., Edinburgh, Scotland

Printed in the United States of America

FIRST AMERICAN EDITION

ISBN 1-84195-625-2

Text design by James Hutcheson

Canongate
841 Broadway
New York, NY 10003

05 06 07 08 09   10 9 8 7 6 5 4 3 2 1

To Karen and
Best Boy Zack

What is our life? A play of passion;
Our mirth, the music of division;
Our mother's wombs the tiring houses be,
When we are dressed for this short comedy.
Heaven the judicious sharp spectator is,
That sits and marks still who does act amiss;
Our graves that hide us from the searching sun
Are like drawn curtains when the play is done.
Thus march we playing to our latest rest –
Only we die in earnest, that's no jest.

On the Life of Man, Sir Walter Raleigh

Cut is the branch that might have grown full
   straight.

Doctor Faustus, Christopher Marlowe

LONDON
29TH MAY 1593

I have four candles and one evening in which to write this account. Tomorrow I will lodge these papers with my last true friend. If I survive the day, they will light our pipes. But should I not return, he has instructions to secrete this chronicle where it will lie undiscovered for a long span, in the hope that when these pages are found, the age will be different and my words may be judged by honest eyes.

Reader, I cannot imagine what future you inhabit. Perhaps the world is a changed place, where men are honest and war, want and jealousies all vanquished. If so, you will wonder at the actions of the players in this poor play of passion. But if you are men like us you may understand, and if you are men like us you will learn nothing, though I gift you the only lesson worth learning, that there is no better prize than life. Whatever the future be, if you are reading this, you read the words of a man who knew how to live and who died an unnatural and unjust death. And what follows is the true record of the circumstances leading to my assassination.

My name is Christopher Marlowe, also known as Marle, Morley, Marly, known as Kit, known as Xtopher, son of a Canterbury cobbler. They say shoemakers' sons go barefoot. It wasn't so bad for us, but my father had a fondness for style that stretched beyond his means and damaged family fortunes. I inherited his tastes, but desired none of his debt, so I have always been in need of money and have risked much where other men might have scrupled.

I was a clever child. My keenness was brought to the attention of a local Knight who sponsored my early education. Years later he would judge me on a murder charge, never meeting my eye though I knew he recognised me well.

When I was seventeen I persuaded an old Archbishop that my one desire was to enter the

Church. He granted me a scholarship to Cambridge University where I was recruited into a strange shadow world, where I was assured I could help my country while helping myself. So it proved and when it seemed my degree might not be granted, due to various absences and rumours which placed me where I shouldn't be, the Queen's own Privy Council gave guarantees I had been on Her business and must not suffer for doing Her good service.

Eventually I moved to London as I always knew I would, and set the world of theatre afire. Men left *Massacre of Paris* with their sword-hands twitching. And when my *Faustus* was performed, some said Lucifer himself attended, curious to see how he was rendered. Yes, it is no vanity to say my plays were a triumph, and Christopher Marlowe so famous they had heard of me in Hell. And so I made shift betwixt two night-time realms and thought my life charmed.

I am of an adventurous nature. I have often invited danger and have even goaded men to violence for the sake of excitement. I like best what lies beyond my reach, and admit to using friendship, State and Church to my own ends. I acknowledge breaking God's laws and man's with few regrets. But if I die tomorrow, I will go to my grave a wronged man. Were this fate of my own doing, I would greet it not gladly, but with a nod to virtue's victory. As it is, if I meet death tomorrow I promise to face him cursing man and God.

★

My story begins on the 19th of May, 1593. All of that month I had been installed at Scadbury, the country house of my patron, Thomas Walsingham. For reasons I will soon explain, it was after noon before I woke, but when I drew back my shutters the day seemed new minted. It was as if I had lighted in another land. A world riven with sunlight. I stood by the window enjoying the lack of London's stink as much as the freshness of the countryside, then repaired to my desk where I worked like the finest of scholars, until the sun edged half the sky and a shadow crept across my words. I let the ink of my last poetry sink into the page and when all danger of smudging was past, locked the manuscript safe in my trunk, slipping one of my own hairs into the clasp, an old precaution, done more from habit than necessity.

It had become my custom to walk in the forest in the early evening. As I write, I search my remembrance, wondering if the weeks cloistered in the country, avoiding the Plague which once more threatened the City, had made me restless. I was used after all to the bustle of theatrical life, London's stews, the half-world of ambidextors and agents. But it seems when I look back on this walk at the end of a perfect day, that it was the most untroubled hour of my life. I didn't know that every step I took was echoed by the beat of a messenger's horse speeding along the London road towards Scadbury. My fate galloping to meet me.

I had much to muse on that late afternoon. The events of the previous night should have been prime in my mind. But I thought of nothing as I walked through the forest. That is, I thought of nothing in particular. Pleasant images threaded through my daydreams: the verses I was engaged on; what might be served for supper; the thighs of a woman I had lain with last winter; the dedication I would compose for Walsingham; how perfect clusters of purple violets looked snug against the forest floor; whether a doublet of the same shade might suit me well. All mingled with contentment at the good fortune of my state. The assurance of my patron's affection, the vigour of my blood, the good reception I felt sure would greet my poetry when I returned at last to London. I see now there was a complacence in my satisfaction and, were I prone to superstition, might suspect I invoked misfortune by displeasing God with my conceit. But such thoughts are nonsense. When making mischief, man needs no help from God or the Devil.

The sun slipped lower beyond the canopy of leaves. The forest's green light deepened, tree shadows lengthened, intersecting my path like criss-crossing staves. I registered dusk's approach and walked through bars of light and dark wondering if I might employ them as a metaphor.

Nature hath no distinction twixt sun and shadow, good and evil.

I saw no one, but the forest was secretly as busy as any London street. Night and daytime creatures crossed, invisible in the gloaming. Birds whistled territorial tunes and small beasts, newly awakened for the night kill, rustled beneath fallen leaves, fleeing my approach. Crickets scratched out their wash-board song and the wind whipped the treetops into a roar. But any crowd has its silent watchers and once I glimpsed the feminine form of a deer, trembling at the edge of my vision.

'That's right,' I said out loud, 'never let your guard down.' Then laughed, because I had let my own guard down, walking unaccompanied through these woods on the verge of night. I remember I paused to light my pipe, trusting the smoke to repel the swarms of midges that hovered around my head, then strode on confident I could reach the house before dark.

So passed my last untroubled moments. I

didn't see the man ride uninvited into the courtyard, hear the familiar clatter of hooves against cobbles, nor witness the manic roll in the eye or the sweat on the flank of the horse driven too fast. But I returned in time to register the customary pomposity of the Queen's Messenger, who greeted me with sarcastic civility and an order from the Privy Council for Christopher Marlowe, playwright, to return to London immediately.

★

Does each escape increase or decrease a man's chances? Each time he wrestles free or weasels beyond charges, does he advance his expertise or merely shrink the portion of his luck?

That I had previously appeared before courts and councils and escaped with only a month or two's incarceration was scant solace as I jolted towards London on a borrowed horse, under arrest again. I recalled a middle-aged swordsman I had once seen confronted with a duel outside a Shoreditch tavern. The man had a reputation as a sword-sharp, but when the bout began, he was ill-equipped to parry what he had once dodged with ease. His opponent's blade had found its mark and the hero of a hundred bouts had folded with a groan, that was more surprise than pain. His killer shouted in triumph. But I knew then that champions' lives are often short and the thought returned now to snatch any comfort previous perils might have granted.

Walsingham had sent ahead to the city to check the messenger's credentials. It had been confirmed he was no conycatcher come to diddle me with a false fine or useless bribe, but the genuine article sent direct from the Privy Council, the most powerful men in the country. Men that can sentence you to death or torture, or to wait your life away, anticipating charges that never arrive. A league who answer only to God, the Queen and each other.

Perhaps it was the rhythm of the horse that turned my mind towards the events of the previous night. But then I have found fear often inspires thoughts of love, and if not love, then lust.

My patron Lord Walsingham is magnificent, well set in every way. Strong-boned and even-featured, his ancestry shows in the ease of his walk, the readiness of his laugh. He ruled our dinner conversations with a charm that belied the steel in his eye. I remembered the other Walsingham, his cousin the spymaster, spider at the centre of a web of intrigue, and watched my words lest my patron had inherited the old man's craft.

We had lived well at Scadbury. I had grown used to fine wines and august company and knew I would be loth to return to the poet's life when my time there was done. The night before my arrest Walsingham and I had dined alone but the table was set for a feast. Spiced capons boiled with oranges, roast lamb and conies, a dish of larks and a salad of cabbage lettuce and rosemary. I didn't mark the composition of the leaves that evening, but reflect now that a maid well versed in the language of flowers would have noted them and realised what was to follow.

Walsingham sat at the head of the table, I on his right hand like some old-world vassal. Dish followed dish, but I noticed Walsingham ate little and drank more than was his habit. I followed suit, matching him cup for cup so by the time the servants removed the plates and were dismissed, we were both drunk, and pleased with each other's company. The night grew darker, the candles burned low and our pipe smoke wreathed the room like old ghosts come forth to join the merriment.

There are moments when an evening shifts from one thing into another. All were abed except we two when the mood turned. Walsingham grasped my shoulder in response to some jest I had made, squeezing it as if in gentle affection but resting his hand against my back, a breath or two beyond propriety. I hesitated, suddenly reduced to my senses, catching the sharp scent of him, hearing the shallowness of his breath. But those who know how to mark the signs, know how to respond. Intoxication tempered surprise. I fathomed him and brushed my hand against his arm, the briefest of touches, to indicate my assent. When Walsingham leaned close and whispered my own lines:

Some swore he was a maid in man's attire,
For in his looks were all that men desire,

I knew how it would go. The time had come to
grant my patron his literary *droit du seigneur*.

When Walsingham straddled my torso,
broad-chested, veiny groin prick-stout, I was
reminded of a back-arching centaur. The image
persisted through the face-fucking interlude that
followed. The smell of sea and sweat and the
conquest of my poetry took place in my head to
the image of a white horse running across hard
wet sands. The rough stabbing of the patron-of-
poetry's cock which jarred this poet's head against
the bed's head took on the rhythm of a gallop,
until the Lord released with a groan, holding his
pulsing prick firm between my lips because somehow satisfaction would not be complete until the
mouth which reads him such fine verse consumed
all Walsingham can give.

Afterwards I stared up at the canopy that
tented the bed, hoping fellow feeling hadn't fled.
My Lord leaned over and ruffled my hair then,

as he dismounted, concluded the verse, making me its hero.

And such as knew he was a man would say,
Marlowe, thou art made for amorous play.

The memory made me smile, though it twisted something like a fist in my belly.

★

I asked the messenger if he knew the cause of my arrest but he gave only a shrug of the shoulders in reply. Twilight shifted into night. The last bird finished its song, leaving the forest to night prowlers and highwaymen. I kept my sword-hand ready. Meanwhile my mind, busy as a late night gaming-board, shuffled through combinations of treason, and my horse carried me ever closer to whatever waited in London.

★

The city rose up before us long before we reached her, a confusion of red roofs slanting this way and that amongst high, pointed spires and smoking chimney stacks. Distance and sunshine made the place look fresh. Farm girls and silly country swains arriving here in search of golden streets must surely rejoice when they first see that view, never suspecting the stews that lie beneath. On Highgate Hill the sails of the windmills turned slowly, but no breeze touched us as we made our way towards the City.

Church bells were ringing as we passed through the city gates. London was as I had left it three long weeks ago when fear of Plague had closed the theatres and I had repaired to Walsingham's house. We made our way towards the river, along roads edged either side by high, timbered buildings which blocked the sun and cast us into shadow. Here rich and poor live one on top of another. Already market traders were setting out their stalls. Milkmaids, muscle-armed and never as fair as the songs suggest, rattled below us, eager to sell their wares before they soured. A mountebank called the afflicted to his remedies and an old fishwife, as high as her catch, cried *Four for sixpence mackerel*. An ancient cove in tattered jester's robes nursed a miserable monkey with a face like a Beelzebub and shouted *Oh rare show!* A pretty country maid sang *Fair lemons and oranges* and I wished we could stop and buy some for their scent, though they were soft and grey spotted. Somewhere tradesmen began to hammer out their day. Sedans, carts and coaches vied for space on narrow roadways already busy with a press of people. London assaulted the senses. The din of voices, superstitious church chimes, pounding mallets, busy workmen and street bustle, undercut by the smells of livings and livestock. My months in the country gave a clarity to my vision and suddenly I felt sure this place could not survive. There was so much energy, so little space. One day the City must surely combust.

Eventually we reached the waterside where the air moved a little freer, though it carried the stench of stagnant places. Beneath the bridge waterwheels groaned like tortured men. And the ill-favoured ferrymen's cries of *Next oars*? seemed like an invitation to cross the Styx. We pressed aboard a barge packed tight with travellers and as we pushed into the swell, the messenger pointed towards a group of strangers gathered on the bank we'd quit. He spoke for the first time.

'Soon there will be no pure English left. Just a mix of Blackamoors and Dutch and God knows what.'

His speech annoyed me and I answered, 'Perhaps the Spanish will relaunch the armada and save us from the deluge.'

But it was an unwise jest; the kind that often escapes my lips when I'm in my cups or lacking sleep and I worried about it for the rest of the journey, fearing I had added to whatever troubles awaited me.

★

'You know why you are here?'

The room I had been called to was plainly

wainscoted in dark oak, relieved only by a tapestry depicting a royal hunt, hung across the
whole of the far wall. I found myself searching it
for the telltale bulge of a hidden listener, but the
arras was set out far enough to comfortably
conceal any spy. Eighteen men faced me, each
dark-dressed with an expression to match. I had
thought I might wait days before being granted
an audience. But relief at being brought straight
into their presence was tempered by the confirmation that my position was deadly serious. This
was the Privy Council. Ministers who cared enough
for high office to profit from death. Who had
committed men they knew well and men they
had met only once to torture and death.
Dangerous men, each with a ruthless core, who
had played chess with their own lives and still
lived, though some had sat in prison cells and
listened to the hollow sound of nails splitting
wood as their own gallows grew in the yard. I bowed
and scanned their faces, recognising the Lords
Cecil and Essex; at opposite ends of the long table,
as far apart in their seating as in their sympathies.

I knew this was not the forum in which to solicit allies, but hoped spymaster Cecil would think me still useful and speak in my support at one of those discreet meetings that take place in dark rooms where alliances are struck and promises exchanged.

The man who had spoken sat at the Council's centre behind a long table of the same gloomy wood that lined the walls. Old and grey with the flinty stare of a survivor, he was an ideal companion to the ancient oak. Destined to grow ever more ancient in the service of the Crown. His gown was black, untrimmed by fur or jewels, but his ruff was intricately pleated, his long beard groomed with a vanity that suggested he had once dressed with more extravagance and might do so again should the age allow. He glanced at the papers before him, then turned his stone stare on me, repeating the question with the patience of one accustomed to completing difficult tasks.

'Do you know why you have been brought here?'

My back ached from the long ride. I concentrated on standing upright, throwing my shoulders back like one of the Queen's livery, though the effort took all my will.

'I thought perhaps the Queen requires my service.'

The old man sighed.

'The Queen requires your loyalty.'

We live in desperate times, where loyalty is all. The Queen grows old. Her allies and her enemies grow restless. Some dread the old religion while others pray for its return. The State is uneasy. It glimpses plots at every turn and fear makes it ruthless. I steeled my voice and met the old man's even stare.

'Loyalty is the duty of every subject.'

He lifted a page from a bundle before him, raising his eyebrows as if something he saw there interested him.

'Loyalty, like love, does not always answer to duty.' He dropped the page and stared into my eyes, lowering his voice the better to emphasise his speech. 'Yours is in question.'

My eyes were drawn to the lace that trimmed the hem of my sleeve. I seemed to see it more clearly than I ever had before. All its wonderful simplicity revealed in a moment. I forced my gaze back to the officials.

'Sir, if there is a question about my loyalty or my love for the Queen, might I be permitted to answer it?'

'Perhaps.' The man's voice was close to a whisper now and all the method that might be employed in the asking was in his smile.

I too know the actor's art. I forced my fear into anger, forging metal into my voice and fixed his eye with a passion that was dangerous in its insolence.

'My loyalty remains steadfast.'

He made an amused fanning gesture like someone trying to banish a bad smell or a small insect.

'We may test you on that promise.'

At the far end of the table a small, squat man took up the questioning. His round, creased face put me in mind of a loaf of bread which, failing to rise, had collapsed back on itself.

'Tell us what you know about the play-wright, Thomas Kyd.'

I turned to face the new speaker, keeping the rest of the Council at the edge of my vision.

'We once shared a patron, Lord Strange, who issued us a common set of rooms. We knew each other, though not well.'

'Master Kyd claims you were once firm friends.'

'Perhaps Master Kyd has fewer friends than I.' I hesitated, but hearing no cock-crow went on. 'I count him an acquaintance. Since I quit the service of our mutual patron we've seen each other only when our paths crossed by chance.'

'Did you ever have him copy work for you?'

'He is a scrivener, son of a scrivener, and makes fine copies by dint of practice. It would not be strange if I had asked him to scribe for me, but I can recollect no occasion when I did so.'

At the far end of the room the tapestry wavered, but whether it was the movement of some concealed listener, or merely in response to a draught as somewhere a door closed, I could not tell.

The man's voice became dangerously intimate.

'So you would deny that a piece of heresy copied in Kyd's hand was initiated by you?'

'I do deny it. I'm accountable for my own writing and blameless of other men's heresies.'

The questioning was taken up from the other side of the table.

'But you are responsible for your own heresies?'

My voice wavered with the effort of freeing contradiction from insult.

'I make no heresies, your Lordships.'

'But there are some who accuse you of being an atheist and attempting to recruit others to the cause.'

'Then they are liars spreading slander.'

'Perhaps,' the new speaker's voice was smooth with a polite disinterest, which belied the sting in his words. 'But your play *Tamburlaine* is known as an atheist tract. It seems strange for a man who is no heretic to write sacrilege.'

'Sir, you know that there are those who dispute our right to have plays at all. *Tamburlaine* was submitted to your Lordships' scrutiny and found to be in accord. Whoever describes it thus casts a slur not just on me but on Her Majesty's Privy Council.'

He ignored my speech and raised a ragged handbill.

'Can you account for this?'

The bill was tattered and torn, it had been roughly pasted somewhere before it was ripped down and delivered to the Council. Traces of the paste used to stick it in place still curled its edges, but the words were clear enough.

> *You strangers that do inhabit in this land,*
> *Note this same writing, do it understand.*
> *Conceive it well, for safeguard your lives,*
> *Your goods, your children, & your dearest*
>   *wives . . .*

> *Your Machiavellian Merchant spoils the*
>   *state,*

Your usury doth leave us all for dead,
Your artifex & craftsman works our fate
And like the Jews you eat us up as bread.

Since words nor threats nor any other thing
Can make you to avoid this certain ill,
We'll cut your throats, in your temples praying,
No Paris massacre so much blood did spill.
——*Signed, Tamburlaine*

'This bill refers to your plays *Tamburlaine* and *Massacre of Paris*, does it not?'

The Privy Council stared at me unblinking, like an audience absorbed in the final act of a thrilling play.

'Sirs, anyone who thinks this my handiwork insults me not simply because of its abhorrent sentiments but because of the ill-formed nature of the verse. If I were to write a libel I would not make it so illiterate. I can only think that this has been contrived with my slander in mind, or by someone who, liking my poetry, has made some misguided attempt to imitate it. It does not reflect my views or my ability. Ask any poet you care to, even one who hates me, and he will tell you the same.'

'We asked Thomas Kyd. He seemed to think it the kind of libel you would relish.'

Even though the knowledge had been with me from the first mention of his name, confirmation of Kyd's betrayal made me flinch. I gathered myself and cast my eyes around the assembly, hoping to impress my innocence on them.

'It is not, but even if it were, I have been away from London this last month.'

'Not so far you couldn't return.'

'Aye sir, but I didn't.'

It occurred to me I could cite Walsingham as witness to my unbroken stay at Scadbury, but I kept silent. Friends do not thank you for Council summons and I realised I was unsure my patron would provide an alibi. My uncertainty came as a revelation and I wondered if Walsingham was as surprised by my sudden recall as he had seemed.

The old man at the centre of the table smiled

his slow smile. His voice took on the monotone of one reciting by rote.

'The Council will be conducting its own investigations. We recognise three charges against you. First that you did request Thomas Kyd copy an heretical tract on your behalf. Second that you are an avowed atheist who has caused others to convert to your beliefs. Third that you did write and paste this libel to the door of the Dutch church, threatening those to whom Her Majesty has offered protection.'

I bowed my head awaiting the instruction to take me to gaol.

'Meanwhile, you are free to go but will report to the Privy Council before noon every day until such time as you are given notice to quit or other measures are put in force.' Here he favoured me with the fond glance of a farmer surveying crops on the eve of harvest. 'You are not under arrest, but failure to report to the Council will result in your arrest. Is that clear?'

I nodded, not trusting my voice.

The official smiled his slow smile again. His

lips were unnaturally red, pumped full of blood behind the white beard. His eyes met mine for an instant. Then he nodded my dismissal and returned to the papers in front of him.

★

Kyd and Kit. The goat and the cat, someone had once called us. But the names didn't stick. They were so plainly the wrong way round. If anyone were the goat then it was I, with my Machiavellian cast and goatee beard. Kyd, on the other hand, had a feline quality. It suddenly struck me that all grace would be racked from him now. The realisation brought tears to my eyes. The world swam and for a while I forgot I was a haunted man. Poor Kyd was a good companion and a fine playwright whose friendship I'd just disowned. I knew he'd understand my denial as I forgave his betrayal, but the weight of bad faith rested heavy in my belly. I wanted to know what had happened to Kyd, needed to know what he had said about me. One place would hold the answers, the destination I most dreaded.

*

Death makes the world a brighter place. I've seen the shape danger gives to things, an edge so sharp that if you like your head atop your shoulders and your entrails tucked safe in your belly it's best not to stop and admire the view. Yet the prospect of death renders everything lovely. Colours shine stronger. Strangers' faces fascinate and your sex calls you to business you must not attend.

We've all seen men swing. Some go pious, strangely eager to meet the Maker who has treated them equal to his bastard son. Others disgrace themselves, shivering, shitting, pleading for a mercy they should know is long fled. Their shame forces me to turn towards the faces of the crowd. Wild-eyed masks, red-faced and spittle spatter- ing, some with appetites so awakened they stuff themselves with pies, meat juices glossing their chins, pastry cramming their mouths, even as they call for the coward to be cut down and quartered. Sometimes though, the condemned have an extra grace. The hangman slips the rope around their necks like a father bestowing pearls on a daughter of whose virginity he is certain. I have watched the wonder on such men's faces and known them to be entranced by the world from which they are about to drop.

From his gallows eyrie, the soon-to-be-dead sees everything. The cheats and pickpockets, the ghouls hoping for a scrap of his clothing, or better still a lock of his hair or a slice of the rope. The condemned hear the clamouring for death. They feel the anticipation of the crowd, as eager as any first-night audience. And who's to say they never want to please the mob? Because, viewed from the gallows, everything is beautiful. The veins on the noses of piss heads glow a blood red shade never witnessed before. And whores whose early corruption has decided the hardened cast of their faces, melt into blameless girls.

Such cursed men surpass Christ. They take a last look at this world and step, still mesmerised by its beauty, into the nothing beyond. They might scream through the ritual of their dis-embowelling, who wouldn't? But more often these are the men who expire before the knife touches their belly, as if by recognising danger's charms they have found the secret of how to die.

It is death that gives a shape to life. Children are conceived in the shade of the gallows tree, new life springing round the roots of assassina-tion. And I too have found myself leaving execu-tions with my prick as hard as a hanging man's. Danger is an intoxicant to trounce tobacco and wine. I should know. I have side-stepped death's scythe more than once. The question is can I do it again?

As always at such times I felt myself to be two men. There was Kit walking through Shore-ditch market, young Kit, tall and strong, creator of *Tamburlaine* and *Faustus*. Kit the atheistic brawler who'd defied a murder charge, who put constables in fear of their life. Kit for whom the crowds part recognising my authority, if not my person. Then there is silent Christopher, watching my progress, calculating how best to hold onto life. Even as I admired myself, a tall young man, chestnut hair swept back from a high brow, pale skin made paler by my fine flame-slashed black doublet, I cursed my misfortune. After the sobriety of the Privy Council it was a relief to plunge into the anonymity of the crowd. But I kept my eyes alert and my sword-hand free. A dagger can find its way into a belly or a back before the victim spies it. I thought I felt the prickle of surveillance on my shoulders. And though I knew it was most likely the effect of my own blood running faster in my veins, I made my way from the crush of people, trying to keep note of who was around me, checking if any faces lingered in the thinning crowd.

★

The turnkey and I were old allies from my time in gaol. I waited by Newgate and got lucky, spying him within the hour. He'd winked to show he'd seen me, then walked on, sure I would

follow, leading me silent down a brackish alley.
We hunched together in a piss perfumed doorway under the cynical stare of a child who knew
the worth of her witness. I moved my hand to
my sword as I tipped her a coin, hastening her
departure.

The gaoler was old, broad-shouldered and
tiny. His stoop concealed his face. When he looked
at me he had to move his whole head sideways.
He didn't look at me often, offering instead the
skelfy view of his bald pate. Pain and profit were
the only colour in the old man's life. He dressed
in dungeon dweller's rags and lived within the
walls of the gaol. Lack of sunlight had drained
his skin of warmth, leaving his flesh with the
transparent gleam of a white slug. I had entrusted
many commissions to his care when I was in clink.
It was an easy matter now to purchase news of
Kyd's ordeal. The old man's hand trembled with
the weight of my angels, he favoured me with an
ecstatic glance and began his tale.

'They brought your friend at the usual time.
In the dark hours between night and morning

when a man is at his lowest ebb and resistance weakest. He held firm until they reached the door of the torture chamber, then spilled all he knew and perhaps a little more.' The gaoler's voice held a relish at Kyd's humiliation. 'They made him sing until he hit the high notes, then they chorused your name and he picked up the refrain.'

I felt sick. Instead of my senses growing accustomed to it, the stench of the alley seemed to grow worse, weaving down into my bowels.

I coughed against the taste of it and asked, 'What was his song?'

'A simple tune. Kyd admitted to copying some seditious claptrap on your behalf. The papers were yours, he said, though they were found in his rooms. He supposed them shuffled with his as a consequence of your living so close for two years.' He chuckled softly at my down-cast look. 'Don't take it hard. He would have sworn the pages belonged to the Lord Jesus Christ himself if it would end the agony.'

'Would that he had.' The irony of the hours

Kyd had spent honing his plots struck me and I laughed. 'When I knew him he sometimes had trouble with his verse. Perhaps I should have threatened him with violence. He seems able to create dazzling fictions when confronted with the rack.'

'Men have no trouble recounting tragedy when it is broken out of them.'

I concentrated on keeping calm.

'How long did it take?'

'Most of the night. He stuck to the story that the papers were yours.'

The anger was in my voice now.

'You spent a whole night on him? Surely you have more interesting subjects in line.'

'Superior playwrights like yourself?' The gaoler laughed. 'The interrogator's art benefits from detail as much as any play. Kyd revealed the plain tale with little encouragement, but any story needs embellishment. How popular would your *Faustus* be if you left out the detail? A magician conjures a devil who then does for him? Facts are fine, but it's detail that makes the plot. As we got to know each other better your friend added intricacies that were worth the wait.'

'What did he say?'

The old man shook his head.

'I've not time to tell you all.' He glanced up at me. I understood and smoothed his hand with another angel. The gaoler nodded convulsively whispering, 'That's good, that's good . . .' like a man close to climax, his hand fluttered about his face then he regained his composure and resumed the tale.

'Kyd talked a lot. Some of it was raving, the usual rubbish men shout on the rack.' He shook his head. 'Some cry for their mothers.'

'Just give me the substance of his words.'

'You were at their centre. An unbeliever who lies with whores of both sexes and accuses Christ, the apostles and John the Baptist of sharing your vice.' He gave me a lascivious nod. 'Tales of your debauching were our bedtime stories.'

'If it were me they wanted, why not come direct?'

The gaoler's voice held contempt for a question he couldn't answer.

'If there's a reason, you're more like to know it than me.' He shrugged and resumed the tale. 'As the night grew darker our friend Kyd seemed sure you had hidden the papers in his room yourself. He said you would do anything for money and thought it likely you were even now enjoying the fruits of his arrest. He called you a double-dealer.'

'I loved him like a brother.'

The old man heard the misery in my voice and looked towards me. The movement twisted his body and for a moment it seemed like he was beginning a gleeful dance.

'He seemed to think you jealous of his writings, a wicked man who would hand his friends to the authorities for gain.'

I put my head in my hands and laughed, though it felt like crying. The old man took me by the arm, his harsh whisper echoed against the silence of the alley.

'Quiet, the very stones are spies.'

I shook my head.

'As if I would so lightly cross a man who spends his days writing of revenge.'

His clawed hand dug deep into my flesh.

'I doubt he'll write much now. Kyd said he thought you bound for Scotland. It might be well for you if he were right.'

'I'll know when it's time to flee.'

The gaoler shook his head.

'You've been in this life long enough to fathom how it works. You're safe as long as they can use you. After that . . .' He hung his head limply to one side, drawing up an imaginary rope, letting his tongue loll from his mouth like a scaffold dancer. 'If you want to stay alive, think on what you can gift them. A man like you can always think of something,' he smiled, 'or someone. There's a particular friend of yours who stands close to the rope. Put his head in it and save your own.'

'Free counsel?'

The old man lifted his head and stared up at me, examining my features as if storing them for future meetings. His face creased into a girn of a grin, crimped lips gummed at the corners with yellowed saliva.

'You seem tall enough to me, but there's always room on the rack if you desire.' I couldn't wrest my gaze from the wrinkled smile. The spit-glued mouth. I placed another coin in the warder's hand. He felt the weight of it, smiling as he accepted it as worthy of his due. 'It's good to gift the turnkey and the hangman, but better still never to meet them.'

'True words. Tell me, what brought them to Kyd's rooms?'

'Don't you know?'

I shook my head. When he spoke the old man's voice held echoes of the torture chamber.

'They thought he might be this new Tamburlaine who pasted the libel to the door of the Dutch church. Some say it should have been you they sent for, but something drew them to Kyd. Maybe some informer, eager for the hundred crowns offered for intelligence of Tamburlaine, maybe something else.' He turned to go. 'Be careful my friend, all roads begin to lead to you.'

We parted, each without a backward glance, leaving by opposite ends of the lane. I felt infected by the stink of the alley, the weight of Kyd's torture and the taint of the gaoler's friendship.

★

The spiked heads of criminals outside the gaol seemed to hold a smile for me alone. Their steady stare put me in mind of a youth I had once glimpsed across a crowded tavern. Neither of us spoke, neither made a move towards the other, but we recognised that there would be congress between us that night. True enough the boy trailed me from the inn and what followed was sweet.

I strode on, leaving the slack grins of the severed heads behind me, but the image of my tongue roving their rotten mouths persisted. The gaoler was right. There were many men I could betray. But probably only one whose life would secure mine, at least for a while. I wondered if he knew of my troubles, if he predicted my thoughts and if he was even now considering whether to stick me before I did for him.

★

The shadows of St Paul's Cathedral cloak books to suit all humours. Poetry, plays, songs and sonnets nestle beside prayer books and improving tales. Fashionable romances, tied with ribbons the shades of ladies' gowns, tumble against masculine manuals and dry theology. Ballads, cheap at half a penny, and clumsy woodcuts, perfect to brighten the bunks of homesick apprentices. Diseases of horse, man, dog and nation. How to raise children or raise the Devil. Descriptions of monstrous things and crimes that stretch credulity. Italian illustrations only gentlemen can view without corruption. It's all there if you know where to look.

The bookshops that edge the churchyard are as different as the goods they sell. Simple booths and shanty stalls hung with pamphlets bracket three-storey tenements stuffed with volumes;

warrens of learning to rival Alexandria. Stationers and print shops are haunted by authors; the humble hopefuls who try to wheedle a copy of their verse between the rollers of the press, the arrogant who lament the ignorance of a trade which rejects, or shifts too few copies to warrant the effort.

Mysterious names painted in pictures swing above each doorway: *The Half Moon* and *The Hand*; *The Holy Ghost* and *Holy Lamb*, *The Bull's Head*, *Bishop's Head*, *Tiger's Head* and *Maidenhead*. St Paul's churchyard is one of the safest places to lose yourself in London. Where grandees and vagabonds, the sober and the foppish, young ladies and old men tread the same paths and no one looks out of place.

The bookstalls which cluster in the centre of the courtyard had been open since seven that morning and now, in mid-afternoon, the strain of the hours was showing on the booksellers' faces. Despite the crowds business seemed slow. The stallholders were all sighs and raised eyes, pursed mouths and pointed looks. They gossiped in low voices amongst themselves, suddenly quitting conversations to hover amongst the browsers.

Casting unspoken curses on those who perused without purchase.

It was Thomas Blaize that I was searching for. My oldest and closest friend and a player who wishes himself a poet. Blaize has published verses that would set dogs howling, could they read. Never satisfied with being amongst the finest of actors, he haunts the literary world hoping to soak talent into his bones and foist his poetry onto readers. Where better to search for my frustrated wordsmith than amongst books? I spied him at last, deep in conversation with a grave and greying scholar and drew close enough to hear the old man bluster.

'I am not obliged to buy a book simply because I put my hand upon it.'

Blaize is long-faced, with large teeth and a high forehead topped by a question mark of a fringe. His dark eyes and high cheekbones have earned him the nickname of the Viper, but it was a satire on his soft nature as much as his dark looks. Now he bared his teeth in a smile and leaned towards the customer.

'I've no quarrel with that.' The smile grew wider as Blaize raised his voice in loud conversation as only an actor can. His words travelled across the churchyard and booksellers and browsers turned towards the commotion. 'There are many fine books in the world.' He turned stage sinister and held up the volume in question, a slim green-bound book of verse I recognised as my friend's sole publication. 'I just wish to know what it was about this particular one that made you discard it?'

The old man took a step back.

'I have already said, it was nothing in particular.' He huffed a little, looking for a reason that might free him of this pest. 'Perhaps it was the colour of the boards.'

Blaize examined the book, raising it to the light, neatly side-stepping a lunge from the ruffled bookseller whose property it was. A few titters echoed around the bookstalls. Other days I would have joined in the merriment, but now I wondered that he could jest with Kyd racked and his closest friend contemplating Newgate. My heart hardened as I watched him appeal to the audience.

'What is wrong with these boards?'

The elderly man took another step backwards, but a small crowd had formed and he found himself hemmed in.

'They're rather dark. I fancy I like a brighter sort of cover.'

He turned to go but the audience were enjoying the show and no one made way for him. Blaize raised his large hands behind the man's back as if, consumed by rage, he was about to grab the ignoramus and hurl him across the churchyard. He lowered his arms with slow theatricality, mugging desperate expressions, emphasising the strength required to restrain himself. The crowd laughed. The elderly man turned towards his tormentor as if scalded, but Blaize was once more composed and complaining.

'I saw you open the volume before replacing it. You perused a page, raised your eyes to the ceiling, then slammed it shut quite abruptly. There was a look on your face, a look of . . .' he hesitated, 'a look I can't describe.'

The man regarded him with exasperation.

'Then perhaps it was the print, it is after all rather small and I am a man of middle years. Or, perhaps it was that the author seemed unable to describe all that he wished.'

The crowd greeted this sally with laughter. Blaize acknowledged his rival's hit, clutching his chest as if mortally wounded.

'Sir,' he said when the merriment had subsided. 'I am going to make you a present of this book.'

The customer backed away.

'I can't accept a gift from a stranger.'

'There is no obligation in accepting a book from its author, except to read it.'

The man looked like this might be the kind of obligation he feared. Someone shouted, 'You've had enough sport from the old fellow. Don't torture him with your poetry.'

There was more laughter and a flash of genuine irritation crossed my friend's face. He recovered quickly and held up a hand against more interruptions.

'Now,' Blaize went on, 'I take it you are a

regular visitor to St Paul's?' The man nodded, tentatively. 'I am also here most days perusing the stalls. When we next meet you can tell me what you think on this book and whether you were wise to so lightly pass it by . . .'

Perhaps he saw me from the corner of his eye or maybe he felt the weight of my stare upon him because Blaize ceased his patter mid-sentence. He turned as if he heard someone call him, then suddenly we were eye to eye.

Kit.

His mouth soundlessly formed my name. I thought I had never seen him so pale and wondered if he was sickening. Forgetting his sport, Blaize pushed through the crowd, coming towards me like a man woken from a dream.

Behind him the stallholder petitioned the elderly man for the price of the poems. The man began to insist the book had been gifted directly to him, by the author himself. The crowd started to disperse as a second, more pedantic argument broke out between the two elderly men.

Blaize kept his eyes on me, unaware of the show behind him.

'I thought you lost.'

'Near enough.'

He put his hand on my shoulder. It was the first friendly touch I'd felt since Walsingham's. I reached towards it putting my hand briefly on his. He glanced at me and I felt his understanding and his fear and regretted doubting his affection. I remembered I might be placing him in danger and said,

'Perhaps we shouldn't be seen together.'

Blaize withdrew his hand.

'Perhaps, but I'm glad you came to me. Come on, there are plenty of places round here where we may be private.'

★

Blaize led me along a damp and leafy lane towards the charnel chapel. I knew where we were headed, Blind Grizzle's. A small, dimly lit concern, run by Grizzle, an ancient bookseller who could no longer see yet plied his wares with an expertise born of memory.

One day, consensus had it, Grizzle would be lamped by some ruffian who would make off with his takings, maybe even the gold he was rumoured to have hidden in some secret place. But, though logic supposed the shop should be beset by thieves, the old man rarely lost a book. He had strung the ceiling of the tiny premises with tinkling bells which trembled as you trod the uneven boards and the floor was scattered with piles of books Grizzle had mapped in his mind, but which often wrong-footed customers. He had a companion, Hector, a clever dog, who marked visitors' comings and goings with a low growl, half welcome, half warning of what would befall anyone foolish enough to trouble his master.

The old man and his dog were the book-sellers' mascot. Held up as an example of canine devotion and triumph over infirmity. And those of his trade rallied to help, though Blaize maintained they were in league with the hound and cheated Grizzle of his best stock right under his sightless eyes. We'd visited the shop together often and knew the old man well, but I wasn't sure of choosing it as a place to exchange confidences. I leaned towards Blaize and whispered,

'Blind men have sharp ears.'

'And tight tongues.' Grizzle turned his unseeing gaze on us. 'Go into my quarters and talk private there if there is something you'd rather I didn't hear.'

'We mean no slight.' Blaize put his hand on the man's arm and I noticed that Hector remained silent. 'Some things are better not heard.'

The old man sighed.

'And yet you bring them to my shop.'

★

The back room was dark and musty, heaped high with volumes. I tripped over something in the gloom and my sword glanced against a column of books. I swore and put my hand towards the teetering pile. It trembled upright for a second, then Blaize laughed and the books tumbled spine

over page into a splayed and jagged mound. The
dog barked and Grizzle shouted, 'Be careful what
you are about. These books are all arranged.'

Blaize returned his call.

'No harm done. We'll sort them before we go.'

There was a grumbling from the main shop,
then the dog and the old man settled and we were
left in silence.

We sat side by side on the bed. Blaize patted
my hand once, but otherwise we didn't touch,
barely looked at each other as we recounted our
bad news.

I spoke first, telling of my sudden summons
from Walsingham's house, my interrogation by
the Council, my unexpected release and the news
of Kyd that the turnkey had given me. I left out
the night-time encounter with my patron, even
best friends should not be trusted with news that
might hang you. Blaize shook his head in disbe-
lief at the outrages in my tale. But when I reached
the end and the gaoler's advice to flee to Scotland,
his mood lifted and he laughed saying,

'Better the gallows than that sorry country.'

I snapped, 'It may come to that.'

And he apologised, though he still smiled as he shook his head. He tagged his apology with an explanation.

'I remained in London the whole of your absence. The Plague put everyone in fear of their lives until Death became a joke to some of us. I joined an alehouse crew who toasted Death each night. And though I never met Him, He graced some of my companions with a visit. I learned to laugh at Death and have not yet shaken the habit.'

I could see Blaize wanted to launch into Plague tales, but I had no time for a litany of deaths and near avoidance. That war was fallow while my danger lurked near at hand. I interrupted him.

'We can reminisce later. I need intelligence of my situation now. Have you any thoughts on the origin of this libel?'

Blaize turned his brown eyes on me and sighed. He rested his elbows on his thin knees then leaned forward, cupping his head in his hand, staring at the floor. His dark hair draped his face, hiding his features as he began to tell me what he knew.

'There were mutterings about you as soon as the libel went up on the door of the Dutch church. To most you were a hero. You know how it goes when Plague is about. Your libel followed rumours that the pestilence does not creep like marsh gas from the ground or float like spores on the air, but is sprinkled through the streets by some foreign hand. Your name was whispered in every tavern and street corner.'

I felt my chest tighten. The Queen's spies are everywhere and street talk can soon lead to a dungeon.

'Did you never think to send for me?'

Blaize shook his head.

'I wanted to relay the rumours to you, but it wasn't so easy. I had no money, no horse and those around me were the same.'

'You could have borrowed money. Stolen a horse. I would for you.'

He raised his head and stared me out.

'You left me in a town stalked by Plague, never knowing when Death might call, while you rested safe and comfortable.' His voice wavered.

'Did it never occur to you that you might return to find me slung into some unmarked pit? Each morning I woke to the clang of the charnel wagons' bells as they lurched through the streets, piled high with the bodies of the dead. You should have seen their load. Men and women tumbled together, old embracing young in poses that would have ruined them in life. Respectable ladies who'd guarded their modesty as rich men guard gold, splayed half naked, their flesh exposed for all the world to see. And children, who only the day before had been their parents' delight, tossed carelessly amongst the rest. The men who drove the carts were drunk and so was I, from morning to night.'

His words stung, but I shook myself free of them.

'I couldn't save you from these trials. Walsingham regards me as a superior servant. He doesn't grant me leave to bring an entourage.'

'Aye, company might spoil his fun.'

I wondered what Blaize knew. We sat in silence for a while, then he continued.

'Anyway, it wasn't so simple. Rumours move like fire. A small blaze begins. You rush to quench it, then when you think you have succeeded and all danger is extinguished, you turn and find its sparks have kindled fresh flames behind you. Before you know it whole buildings are ablaze, then streets.' He shook his head at the inferno he had conjured. 'Anyway, people thought you guilty of slandering the immigrants, but they praised your guilt.'

I could imagine Blaize at the centre of some ale-house debauch, relishing the attention that association with my notoriety brought.

I hissed, 'Blaize, these are times when we must all tread careful.'

He straightened in his seat and turned towards me, incredulous I should consider him disloyal.

'I spoke only in your defence.'

'Aye, but what kind of defence was it? That I was fearless and would stop at nothing? That because I had written *Tamburlaine* I was as reck-less as my hero?'

'Nothing so rash.' Blaize rose from the bed

and stood facing me. 'Do you think Tamburlaine a name I speak lightly?'

★

I had always been half in love with Tamburlaine, my most ruthless creation, a savage Scythian shepherd-made-king who acknowledged no obstacle in his campaign of conquest. I had felt him at my shoulder as I wrote, pushing my quill to further outrage.

Tamburlaine had been a triumph, though some considered it damned. It was too unnatural, this viciousness that refused to be mastered by good. And it was true that there had been a cursed quality about the production from the first, a curse that had touched my friend and given him good reason to hate my hero.

Blaize had been one of *Tamburlaine*'s principal players. On the opening night he'd realised his pistol contained real shot just as he squeezed the trigger. Somehow he had swerved his aim, desperate to avoid his fellow actors, but instead of pointing at the rafters or to the floor, he'd wheeled the barrel towards the crowd who hardly had an instant to gasp, before the retort had sounded, thunderous even over the hubbub of the theatre, so loud that for an instant all were deafened. Then hearing was awakened by screams. Some thought themselves shot who were just shocked, others that the Spaniards were upon us. But when the confusion abated it was discovered that disaster had occurred. The shot had injured a man and killed a woman large with child.

Guilt had haunted Blaize for a long time. Indeed, thinking on it now I wondered if he had ever got over the calamity. It seemed to me that after the accident his work had taken on a desperate turn. And since that time he often looked as if the shot still rang in his ears.

I patted the bed beside me and said, 'I know you meant me no harm.'

Blaize sat and I rested my hand on his shoulder hoping my touch would reassure him as his had comforted me.

'There's only one way to save myself. I must

find this person who calls himself Tamburlaine and put his head where he would put mine. In a rope necklace.'

★

Grizzle asked, 'Did you sort those books you jumbled?'

And we told him, 'Aye.' Though they were scattered across the floor of his stockroom like a booby trap.

He'd known us liars and complained, 'You take advantage of me. No doubt half my stock is under your arm, just as half my gold is with your creditors.'

I looked at Blaize and he twirled his fingers, aping madness. As we walked away from St Paul's, I caught him fingering a vellum-bound volume. He met my look and smiled.

'Something I found amongst the cheap stalls.'

I stared hard and evil at him, then we both laughed, pleased to be back in each other's company. Still, I hoped that for once Blaize was telling the truth, because I couldn't shake the feeling that to rob the blind man would be to invoke misfortune.

★

These days new ale-houses spring from the bones of old, so fast it is barely worth learning their names, if names they have. There are so many unlicensed places. Inns not consecrated by bush or painted sign. Ale-houses that draw the initiated through their doors by secret badges, a red lattice or a chequered board. Blaize and I were in search of such a place. Somewhere near the Dutch church and the start of my troubles. A tavern where drink was cheap and loose talk might reveal news of my nemesis.

Our journey was accompanied by the constant clanging of church bells, a sound that plagues our city, so regular Londoners ignore the peals. But that day it seemed impossible to shut them out. Each chime jolted my bones as if they marked out my last hours. As we walked, I considered shaking loose of Blaize. But he had scented the angels in my pocket. And there was something in me that wanted to keep him close. Maybe I was tired of being alone, maybe I felt safer knowing where he was. Whatever the reason, we were yoked together that afternoon. I told myself a man in company strikes up conversation with strangers more easily than a lone fox and kept Blaize near.

At last we found a rough, dark place, a cave of a pub crowded with men. The din of their talk stretched into the street. A deep rumble rising to crescendos of laughter and dispute. The occasional woman's voice climbed above the men's, piercing the low babble with boozy shrieks. As we entered the smoke-scented gloom, I recognised it as a nest where poor men and rich rogues sup together, searching for the deliverance alcohol can give. I felt my spirits lift. It was a kind of coming home and I realised I would delay justice for the sake of a good drink.

In the corner a hump-backed fiddler scraped out a tune that was more counter chord than true. He met my eye, then lowered his gaze to his bow, moving with the music. Two Africans in tattered livery, their skin faded from black to grey, slumped together over drinks, click clacking in their own tongue, planning escape or maybe reminiscing on sunshine lands. The tavern was one step up from a cunny-warren and fostered women to suit most tastes, buxom and thin-boned, stern-silent feigning sober, jolly drunkards who shivered their breasts towards you for a draught of Spanish wine, or something less fine. And if you wished another kind of company, the means to detect it would be here.

Spies are advised to stay sober. A little alcohol may sharpen the wits but too large a dose kills judgement. It helps the flyest fail, renders the slyest stupid and apt to let slip secrets. It makes us careless of codes, a poor fist in a fight. It helps us forget what we need to remember. Spies are warned not to fog their senses. They need the concentration of tightrope walkers, the keen eye of an archer.

I knocked back a cup of ale and then another. Blaize followed my example and soon we were three cups down and the strain of the last day was easing. I had met a thousand near-deaths through drink, and felt the pull towards one more. I just hoped it wasn't a dress rehearsal for the real thing. We were on our fourth cup when Blaize reached into his jerkin and drew out a small envelope.

'I forgot to give you this.'

The fiddle sounded low. A woman gave a high laugh as she left the tavern on the arms of two men. I hesitated over the anonymous seal, noting it was unbroken.

'What is it?'

Blaize shook his head but I persisted.

'Where did it come from?'

'A boy passed it to me a week or so ago.' Blaize swilled back his drink and wiped his mouth on the back of his hand. 'He came into the tavern where I was drinking, asking for me by name.' He adopted the faltering voice of a nervous youth, '"Thomas B-B-B-Blaize actor, friend of Christopher M-M-M-Marlowe,"' here Blaize made a comic flourish, '"p-p-p-p-p-playwright of this parish."'

I thought at first it must be some message from you, but when I identified myself he asked whether I would be willing to deliver this. I saw no harm and accepted it as a favour.'

He downed the last of his drink and called for more. I hesitated, unsure why I was so reluctant to fracture the wax.

'Did you ask the boy who sent him?'

'A stranger who offered him a farthing, I added another for his trouble and sent him on his way.' Blaize laughed, toasting me with his refreshed glass. 'I won't trouble you for the return of the coin.'

I gave him a weak smile and unfastened the envelope. Inside was a piece of plain white linen. I turned the scrap over in my hands for a moment as if hoping its unmarked surface hid some trapped communication, which would warm and reveal itself to the heat of my palms. I looked at Blaize and he took it from me, examining both sides, searching for something I might have missed. He shook his head and returned the strange message.

'Some obscure jest?'

I stuffed the envelope into my jerkin.

'Which comes fast on threats to my life.'

'No,' he smiled with relief. 'It was given to me before you returned home, prior to this adventure.'

I took the scrap of fabric from my pocket and held its blank face to him.

'Perhaps it's a comment on my writing. The sender thinks my work empty?'

Blaize laughed, his large teeth seemed to shine in the gloom of the bar.

'Aye, no doubt it'll be something like that.'

'Nonetheless I'd rest easier if I knew who it came from.'

'And I wish I had a secretary to mind my business.'

I flicked at his ankle with my scabbard. He dodged the blow and bumped a fellow standing behind him, splashing the man's drink onto the floor. He was an old scurvy peasant and we out-stared his annoyance until he grumbled into a corner with the dregs of his drink and we forgot the message in the next round of ale.

I cast my gaze around the bar wondering who best to fall into conversation with. I was hoping for a group of men whose confidences could be bought with drink and wit. But my eyes were drawn to a lone stranger. A small man in black hose and doublet, with a cape of the same shade lined in red. His face was indistinct, hidden in the tavern shadows and the broad brim of his hat, but I could make out deep watchful eyes and a grey goatee beard. I thought he might pass for the Devil and smiled to myself, for had Old Nick requested my soul in exchange for earthly peace I would have obliged and thought him the worse for the bargain.

I nudged Blaize and said, 'That cove seems over interested in us.'

Blaize looked behind him.

'He's about to fall into his cups and stares at us for some focus.' He laughed. 'The serving girls ignore him. You and I are the North Star that will guide him to the bar and another drink.'

My friend was usually shot through with suspicion and I wondered at his new-found tolerance. I shook my head.

'It's more than that.'

I glanced back at the man, but he'd scented he was at the centre of our discussion and began to rise unsteadily from his seat, his sword tangling him lewdly like a third leg. Blaize laughed at the man's awkwardness. But pretending you're unfit to handle a sword is a trick as old as Adam. The stranger's clumsiness put me on edge and I felt my hand drifting towards my weapon.

Blaize noticed and whispered, 'Think before you start trouble.'

'If trouble comes looking, it will find me.'

'Aye,' he hissed, 'and you'll be as pleased as a dog in a doublet, until you find yourself in clink.'

Any player will tell you it is hard to fake drunkenness. The man staggered a little as he stepped towards us and I thought his acting over-done. He noted my hostile stance and tut-tutted, raising his arms in mock surrender. Some men at a nearby table spotted him for a soak and laughed, drunk themselves, but sharp enough to relish another's humiliation. The man paid them no mind and continued corkscrewing towards us. As he stepped from the shadows I could see the ravages drink had wrought, the broken nose skewed half across his face, the scarred mouth sliced in drunken descent against the rim of a tavern table, the deep lines that long restless nights had etched around his eyes. I remembered talk from France, that he had been subjected to the strappado and wondered less that I hadn't recognised him. If Richard Baynes was the Devil, he was as tormented as any of his subjects. He offered us a black-toothed smile.

'Is this how you greet admirers?'

I felt Blaize's pride twitch. A peacock's tail that might unfurl full fan if coaxed. Baynes bent into a bow that almost toppled him. Blaize nodded, graciously accepting the salute. But it was not Blaize that Baynes' dark tunnelled eyes looked on. It was me.

'Master Marlowe, your plays do well.' His voice was thick with drink. 'I think of late you have given me as much pleasure as my wife and with none of the aggravation.' He dissolved into merriment at his own wit. 'I'd be honoured if you'd join me in a drink.' He caught the barmaid's eye and signalled deftly for three refills. 'A toast to theatre.'

Blaize drained his draft in one long gulp, hiding his expression behind his cup. He set the empty vessel back on the bar, then wiped his mouth on the back of his hand. When he spoke, his voice was laced with perfect patience.

'So, you know each other well?'

'Tolerably.'

I thought back to the little Dutch town of Flushing where we had shared a room until Baynes, unnerved by the business in hand or hoping for preferment, I was never sure which, accused me of coining and blasphemy. I'd counter charged and we'd been dragged back, under guard, to London, both of us guilty and unwilling to hang. Though it should have made me cautious, the memory was reassuring. I'd faced disaster before and lived to meet it over again. I might yet survive to hang another day and this faithless spy, who'd played the priest for both sides, who slid and slipped through the darksome edges of several cities, might be the key to unlock Tamburlaine.

Baynes gave me a wink designed to exile differences to the past and raised his cup toasting our friendship, unsure of Blaize and ready to slip with espionage ease into any role assigned. I lifted my own drink, returning the salute. The rims of our cups touched and our eyes met. I smiled that I could think him Lucifer; he was at worst a minor Devil, inclined to wickedness but without the wit to execute it unaided.

'Master Baynes is an habitué of the theatre.'

'I visit as often as I can.' The little man beamed at Blaize.

'He likes its twists and turns, though sometimes it can frighten.'

'Aye, I have been frightened near to death on more than one occasion.'

Blaize knew we spoke in riddles but could not fathom our purpose.

'Sometimes I wonder that we call them plays,' he ventured.

Baynes spluttered on his drink.

'True enough, it often seems no game.' I gave Richard Baynes a warning look, not wanting Blaize tangled in the kind of affairs with which this imp concerned himself. He caught my meaning and changed tack, asking Blaize, 'And you, Sir, are you also a writer?'

'I'm better known for treading the boards.'

'It's a wonder I have never seen you. But no mind, we have met now and that calls for further libation.'

I stepped in to retrieve my friend's reputation.

'This man is one of the finest players in London.'

Blaize scowled at my speech. His Adam's apple bobbed as he gulped back more ale. Baynes appeared immune to his distress. He laughed and clapped the finest player in London on the back better to stir the pot of his hubris.

'Then I have most definitely seen you. It's just that I don't remember!'

Blaize's darkening looks, bitter as an abandoned bride's, should have warned me, but when

Baynes dismissed Blaize and returned to me demanding, 'Now what about your poor damned Faustus?', I found myself laughing at his attentions and the actor's distress.

Baynes slammed the surface of the table. Our drinks trembled in their cups, miniature oceans on the edge of a storm.

'Could he not be saved? Zounds! Surely God would be merciful to such a learned man?'

In these times when men turn the talk to religion, it is safer to draw it to something else, like their mother's whoring, their father's cupidity, children's stupidity. Better to compare his sister's breasts and holiest parts with his wife's, than discuss Christ or the apostles. I knew to be beware of Baynes and his like. He and I had fished for traitors in our younger days using blasphemies for bait. We were the same kind of men. And that should have been warning enough. Yet, who understands you like your twin? The room swam and I was at one with the tavern dwellers, the prostitutes and sinners. I was with my own kind and this low place suited

me better than all of Walsingham's luxury and
Ralegh's philosophising.

Baynes swore on Christ's wounds and I
answered, 'God abandoned his own son. Why
should he be more merciful to Faustus? They
weren't even close kin.'

'No,' the little man wagged a finger at me,
and though his words were pious his tone was all
dissent. ''Twas the Jews killed Christ. The same
dark race as pollute our land now.'

It was nothing I hadn't heard before and my
retort was well rehearsed.

'The Jews were his own folk and knew him
best. They had the choice between Christ and
Barrabas and chose Christ, though Barrabas was
a thief and a murderer. I can only suppose Christ
deserved all he got, though being the bastard son
of a whore, it's no surprise he turned out bad.'

I placed my pipe between my teeth and
started to light it. Baynes shook his head, his
clever grin caught in the light of my flame. His
eyes gleamed red, like a devilish cleric coaxing an
inverted catechism from a new wrested soul.

'You can't think it so.'

I took a draw and puffed smoke into his face.

'Oh I do.' I was enjoying myself now. 'The angel Gabriel was but a bawd to the Holy Ghost. Did he not solicit Mary and was not Christ the result?'

Baynes feigned shock.

'But Christ gifted us the sacraments. He made us safe in God's love.'

'An evil love that requires his own child's blood as sacrifice.' I forgot my mission to discover Tamburlaine. The drink had lifted my senses until I delighted in the kind of blasphemies that set sober men reciting prayers or singing hymns, because it is unsafe even to think these truths. I stared Baynes in the eye and whispered, 'If Christ had any sense he would have made more ceremony of the sacrament. The papists have the best idea. They know the theatre of religion. They make a spectacle of the thing. I'd rather watch a show by some papist priest with a shaven crown than a hypocritical Protestant ass.' Blaize laughed, goading me to further outrage. 'Christ

knew nothing of theatre. Better he should . . .'
I took another pull of my pipe searching for inspiration. '. . . Better he should praise God with tobacco than wafers.'

I raised my cup to the room and felt all-powerful, cursing Christ and his vengeful father to a man dressed in the Devil's colours.

Baynes hissed, 'But surely as a man of letters you must love the Bible. Is it not the finest book ever written?'

If I had been sober, I would have marked he slurred less now than before. But the thrill of drink and danger was on me. I laughed and told him it was filthy done and were it up to me I would much improve its style. My tomfoolery cheered Blaize, though he had heard it all before. He laughed and coaxed me on.

'Tell him what you think about the apostles.'

And so it went, I spinning blasphemies, Blaize encouraging my outrages and the small man remonstrating irony as he fed us ale, until he emptied his purse, the night drew dark and we sallied into the street.

Blaize reeled down the alley and stood against the wall, muttering to himself as he fiddled with his codpiece. His mumbles ceased and I heard the splash of his stream hiss against the wall. He sang softly as he pissed. A child's lullaby. For some reason the song lowered my spirits. I rallied all my optimism and slung an arm around Baynes, declaring him my new brother and all past differences forgot. The small man returned my hug and I thought him full of filial love. Then the mood changed. His body stiffened and I realised his small frame was more vigorous than I'd supposed. Suddenly he was pressing his poniard into my waist, letting me feel its point, pushing hard enough to pierce my doublet, but no further. He held my arm in a lock I would not have believed him capable of. Then he put his face close to mine and I thought I smelled a whiff of sulphur. I gasped against the shock of his attack, gathering my breath to call for Blaize. But Baynes pressed the knife deeper, piercing my flesh, slicing a cut along my side, stopping, but promising more should I make a noise. For a full second the street was silent save for our ragged breaths and the sound of Blaize's stream. Then Baynes spoke. His voice rasped, full of hatred and disgust, so different from the smooth tones that had eased blasphemies from me.

'You're a wicked man. Make your peace before you die. Your time is coming soon.'

He spat on my face and pushed me away. His footsteps rang slow and insolent into the dark streets beyond. The drink heaved within me and I bent over on the roadside, retching into the gutter. When I turned, sword in hand, ready to stick him through, Baynes was nowhere to be seen.

★

Blaize weaved from the alley just as Baynes's steps died into silence. He tucked himself safe within his breeches, laughing at my distress, then flung his arm under mine. His touch came too fast on Baynes's betrayal and I struggled against him. But he held me upright, half crutch half rudder, steering me I knew not where. He staggered and fell, pitching me forward. I heaved again and felt my head grow clearer, though my heart felt sick with stupidity and fear. Blaize struggled to his feet and misreading my dread for melancholy said, 'I have a room nearby and on the way we will collect a cure for your malaise.'

★

I watched as Blaize undressed the girl, unfastening her bodice, being gentle with her for she was rightly nervous at being alone with two men. I started to strip myself. We had visited this vice before. I knew how it went and could think of no better way to lose myself than this further degradation.

The girl's body shone silver in the darkness. Blaize presented her to me like an unwrapped gift. She smiled bravely, she had decided he was safe, but I was an unknown quantity, silent and stern while he was all tickles and smiles.

I placed my palm on the small of her back, pulling the girl towards me. She let herself be drawn, but there was enough resistance to let me know she was still unsure or perhaps she thought it might excite me.

'How now, Mistress Minx?' I whispered. 'I would that we had a light.'

And she pushed herself against me, rocking against the hardness she felt there. I put my face in her hair, smelled smoke and evening air and heard her say, 'We will make sparks by moonlight.' And felt better. It was such an old phrase that I knew she had said it to other men and I was not the destroyer of her innocence. I ran my fingers softly around the curve of her rear, over the swell of her thighs, into the swoop of her waist. The contrast between her soft round flesh and my stiff arrow straightness was fascinating. I wished we had a glass, so I could see us side by side, watch my body merging into hers. I dipped my head to her throat, pushed a finger inside her, then rubbed her wetness against her nipple and pressed it to my mouth. She gasped, hooking her

legs around my waist, helping me guide myself within her, clasping her hands around my neck. I placed my palms to her rear, leading her into a rhythm that had us both gasping until the strain became too much and I lowered her to the bed, covering her with my body. Conscious all the time of Blaize's smile in the gloom.

When we had finished and began to draw apart I felt the return of her nervousness and understood she knew this was the dangerous time, after the act, the moment men often turned and did harm to women. I stroked her hair in re-assurance and looked towards Blaize. He shook his head and threw me a coin. It twinkled as it shot through the dark. I caught it and gave it to the girl, adding two of my own. Her relief hung in the air as she quickly dressed herself, eager to leave. When the door had shut behind her Blaize hissed, 'You might go to Hell for this.'

The liquid dark embraced us both. I whispered, 'Hell is on this earth and we are in it.'

His breath stroked my face, he reached towards me, then we were together. Sometime in

the night I woke to the sound of sobbing. But whether it came from the street, or within my head I could not say.

★

Where else can a poet live but the bastard sanctuaries? Beggars' breeding grounds where all are as welcome, or unwelcome, as the other. My lodgings are in a broken-up tenement in Norton Folgate. It was here that I headed, plunging into a bright new morning breezed through with the stink of the Thames.

It was early by theatrical standards but the streets were already swarming with the need to make a coin. I crossed the bridge, travelling against a tide of travellers who were bound for the shore I had just quitted. A parade of people who, having nothing to sell, sold themselves. Jugglers and tumblers; coiners, cutpurses and cosiners; dancers, fiddlers, nips and foists, vagabonds of all description. Three generations of rogues swelled the throng. Ragged children studying the moves of apprentices and masterless men. Old soldiers, who were soldiers no more, just shuffle gaited beggars nursing their sores. All were making their way to the City from the night-time sanctuary of privileged places.

Prominent amongst their ranks were the strangers. Those who, finding no sympathy in their own country, had sought out ours, bringing with them their own ways and customs and sometimes an expertise the Queen wished to claim for her own. They were unpopular amongst the people. The incomers' differences and skills inspired jealousies and mistrust that resulted in attacks, woundings, murder and dissent. The Crown had countered with statutes promising harsh measures against anyone offering harm to strangers and promising the ultimate sanction of death. The paper the Council had shown me had taken my writings and implicated me in a rough plot against the newcomers for which I might be hung.

Come dusk the traffic would reverse direction. And as the night grew dark so would creep the respectable rich and poor following in the rogues' wake. Burgesses, merchants and aristocrats, esquires and gentlemen, stepping from the city into the unchartered quarters, heading for the bear-baiting pits and playhouses. Hunting for the company of harlots, whores and sixpenny strumpets. Bewigged and bedazzled they would drop their breeches in bawdy houses, thanking God for inventing a sin they would regret and renounce even before they had returned to the safe side of the river.

In the midst of the crowd someone shouted, 'Look to your purse!' Most were wise to the old ruse and kept their hands clear of their money. Near to me though a youth in velvet breeches clutched at the chest of his jerkin, nicely marking the thief's target. A one-legged man vaulted past, nimble on one crutch, jolting the youth as he went. A second cripple followed in the first's shadow, a legless long-armed rogue birling fast on a box fixed with rollers. Each man bore the leery marks of boxing bouts. In an instant the boy's purse was snatched and passed and the thieves absorbed by the crowd. No one offered sympathy. London hands out such lessons by the minute and it is up to each to look to himself.

Every fourth door led the way to a tavern or ale-house, every fifth to the house of a bawd. The interview with the Council still hung heavy on me. I wondered at it coming so fast on Walsingham's attentions, but dismissed my suspicions. What we had done was a capital offence, but neither could implicate the other without incriminating himself and he could easily be free of me without recourse to law or murder.

I turned my thoughts instead to my destination, wondering if my rooms remained free. I'd paid my landlady two months' rent on the eve of my departure. She'd been in her quarters frying chitterlings. The chopped intestines had wriggled like grubs, bouncing and snapping in their own fat, filling the room with the sick-sweet smell of burning hellhag. She'd turned to face my knock on the open door with her usual sour expression. But my promised absence and the sight of so much coinage had wrought a transformation. The landlady had tested each bit with her teeth then gripped my arm in a nightmare hold, with hands even harder and more wrinkled than her face. She'd invited me to eat with her and, not offended by my curled lip refusal, began her feast, tripping forth a series of rusty smiles punctuated by chews, swallows and assurances about the cleanliness and security of my chambers.

But in a world where men are cuckolds, a faithless landlady might rent out the bed of an absent tenant. Had my return been more auspicious I would have swashbuckled into the lodgings ready to repel all comers, but that day the thought of discovering some decayed gentleman amongst the few things I'd stored there was repulsive. Worse, if Kyd's rooms had been ransacked, my own might have received the same treatment. Who could know what awaited me there? I ducked into a tavern across the street from my quarters, a mean low-ceilinged place that suited my mood. The main trade would arrive later in the day when men had worked up a thirst or crawled from their beds, but there were a few drinkers sitting in the shadows nursing their ale and their pipes at rough wooden tables decorated with the uneven chips and random scorings of careless men. I ordered sack, commissioned a boy idling by the door to deliver news of my arrival and a request that my rooms be made ready, then settled myself in a dark corner with a good view of the door. In the centre of the room a group of men were playing chance. The clack of their dice and low definite calls of their bets was the only noise within. The randomness of the numbers was soothing against the regular tumble of the dice. I sipped my drink and allowed myself to drift with the sound.

The events of the previous days came back to me. The long journey from Walsingham's house, the interview with the Council. I recalled my patron's power, wondering again if the turn our last night had taken would do me harm. Finally I fancied myself back in the peace of the forest. Recalled the intricate construction of ferns that flourished in the sylvan depths. Each with its own space, all their world supremely arranged. And yet these curling miracles were ruthless. Any unfurling too close to another or happening to fall too deep in the shade, would wither without hope of assistance.

My musings were interrupted by the return of the boy with the news that my rooms had been ready 'these past six weeks'. I detected the injured innocence of my landlady's voice in these words. And nodded the boy's dismissal. Instead of leaving, he proffered an envelope.

'She asked me to give you this letter which arrived for you an hour ago.'

I gave him the coin promised and another to acknowledge the untampered seal on the envelope. He lingered, hoping to be commissioned with a reply, but I sent him on his way with a look.

My urge was to save the envelope for a more private place, but even if it contained bad news, it was best to know before braving the street. I held the missive beneath the table, broke its anonymous seal, tore open the envelope and drew out a small square of scarlet linen the same shape and cryptic blankness of the virgin fragment Blaize had given me the previous day.

If it hadn't been for the interview with the Council, the meaning of the strange messages might have eluded me until much later. But suddenly it revealed itself. I tossed back my drink and exited the tavern, shoving the blood-red note into my pocket, pulling my cloak about me as I went.

★

My room was as mean and dark as I remembered. I sat on the bed and took the pieces of linen from my pocket. Lines from *Tamburlaine* came to me and I whispered them out loud.

> *The first day when he pitcheth down his tents,*
> *White is their hue, and on his silver crest,*
> *A snowy feather spangled white he bears,*
> *To signify the mildness of his mind*
> *That, satiate with spoil, refuseth blood.*

My hands clenched into fists. I uncurled them and watched the crushed fabric unfold, trampled roses, one as red as the other was white.

Tamburlaine had decked his siege camp in three successive shades. First white, offering peace should the enemy surrender. Next red, indicating the execution of all combatants. Finally black, promising death to every last man, woman and child. Not even a dog would survive the slaughter.

The Privy Council had no need for these games. Tamburlaine was my best, most invincible hero, he had lent me some of his power and I never felt as good as when he walked invisibly by my side. His boast came back to me.

I hold the fates bound fast in iron chains.
And with my hand turn fortune's wheel about;
And sooner will the sun fall from his sphere
Than Tamburlaine be slain or overcome.

Tamburlaine the Great remained unvanquished to the last, reducing all in his path to rubble. But

I was his creator and would outdo any angry God. I would destroy my creature turned enemy, just as soon as I knew who he was. I lay back on the bed, closed my eyes and slept, the scraps of linen growing damp in my curled palm.

★

The knock wasn't my landlady's tentative tap, but an authoritative rapping which brought to mind the Queen's Messenger and set my heart racing. Bidding the visitor, 'Wait one minute,' I put my eye to the crack I had contrived in the doorjamb long months ago when I had first rented the rooms. The sliver wasn't wide enough to reveal the whole man. Just an impression of brown leather jerkin and russet breeches. The figure moved, blocking the view as if he knew he was being watched. I kept my hand on my dagger and opened the door quick onto a stranger. He saw my combative stance and took a step back, making it clear he wished me no threat, but smiling as if amused I should think myself any match for him.

'Master Marlowe?'

I nodded.

'I represent someone eager to meet you.'

The man in front of me had the dimensions of a smallish oak. Though his bulk might hamper his swiftness, his strength would more than compensate. I guessed he wasn't inviting me for a feast and bought time by wilfully misunderstanding him.

'I appreciate the invitation, but I have many other obligations.' I gestured towards the open door. 'Bid your master good health and thank him for his compliments.'

He looked around impatiently.

'We have no time for disputing. Make haste, my master requests you come to his house where you will hear something to your advantage.'

'Your master's name?'

'Is not for casual ears.' He shifted impatiently. 'I assure you no harm awaits. Though harm will certainly find you, should you refuse my invitation.'

The unavoidable moment where I hit him

and he knocked me around the room before taking me where he had always intended was fast approaching. I took a deep breath and hoped it wouldn't hurt too much. I made a flourish towards the open door.

'I would rather you accept my invitation and leave.'

He laughed.

'Master Marlowe, I wish you no ill. But I have instructions to make sure you reach my patron's house and reach it you will, alert or sleeping. You choose the way.'

It is suicide to start a fight with a superior opponent in a small space. Especially if your enemy is in front of the only door. I put my hand to my sword.

'Be careful,' he said, 'a sword once drawn is difficult to sheathe.'

And though I knew the truth of his state-ment, I found myself drawing the weapon from its scabbard and lunging towards him in a clumsy thrust not illustrated in any manual of swordcraft.

He side-stepped my attack, surprising me

with his nimbleness, parrying my moves with three successive strokes each of which was a near strike until I was against the far wall and at his mercy. He kept his sword at my throat and knocked me a quick punch to the jaw with his fist. The blow drew a little blood and shook my brains around, though not enough to knock sense into them. He pressed the point to my Adam's apple, gentle but firm enough to let me know the skin would soon break, then withdrew his blade and gave me a grin.

'Ready?'

I shook my head to clear the sound of bells, then nodded to stop him hitting me again.

'Good,' he smiled indulgently as I dabbed the blood from my face. 'All is well, Master Marlowe. Remember, men's interests don't always lie at odds.'

Which is true, but then he didn't know what my interests were.

★

We travelled in a windowless carriage, hurtling along the uneven roads at a bewildering speed, which soon had me disorientated, though I began the journey calculating streets and turnings, half expecting to be bundled across the river. When we arrived, I was harried quickly, not with a rag or cap about my face, but wedged so tight between the coachman and my companion that I was blinkered and could make out only the impression of a formidable town-house.

The room my new friend ushered me into was modest, an anonymous office which offered no clues about the nature of the person who worked there. A man of about thirty was seated behind a large wooden desk. He was small, more elf than gnome, with a clever, pointed face. He would have looked youthful were it not for his dark hair, which receded sleekly into a widow's peak giving him a sinister aspect. He looked up, then signed something with a flourish and came out from behind the desk.

'Master Marlowe, thank you for agreeing to visit us. May I offer you a drink?'

I could have said they left me no choice. But there seemed little point. So instead I bowed and asked for wine. The man nodded to my chaperone who, reduced to the role of steward, poured us both a glass of malmsey before bowing and retiring. I had trusted his openness and was sorry to see him go for I could tell that the man in front of me was of a more sophisticated cast. We settled ourselves in adjoining seats and sat for a while in silence. My companion leaned back, steepling his hands beneath his chin, button-bright eyes examining me as if there was something he couldn't quite decide upon. I sipped my drink quicker than I meant to, and waited for the reason for my visit to be revealed. At last he spoke.

'You seem to find yourself in some small difficulty, Master Marlowe.'

'It is a fact of my profession. Theatre is built on difficulties.'

'The theatre of life also?'

'It is so for all men.'

'Perhaps,' he smiled, a brotherly smile, sympathetic, yet with no illusions about my character, 'but most men's troubles are of a mundane nature. They lack money or have upset their wife. You are in danger of losing your life.'

I took a swig from my glass and returned his grin.

'That has the ring of a threat.'

'It's a fact. The city is unnerved by Plague and on edge with the threat of war. The Spanish are rumoured to be outside our ports. Only yesterday the Queen dispatched troops to way-lay invasion. Times are desperate, tempers stretched and the Privy Council is investigating you. Should investigations go badly, you might swing.'

And that is only the half, I thought. For though I feared the Council, Tamburlaine had been at the forefront of my concerns. I banished doubt from my voice.

'I have confidence in the Council's ability to find the truth.'

He laughed. 'Master Marlowe, you know as well as I that the Council finds what it seeks.' He took a sip of his drink and turned serious. 'Has it occurred to you to wonder why you are not locked safe and tight in Newgate?'

The sound of a key turning in a lock and a poor view through a barred window had been my constant expectation since returning to London. But there was no premium in admitting it.

'I thought perhaps some influence or friendly feeling had worked for me amongst the Council.'

He leaned forward, like an eager schoolmaster congratulating a poor student on mastering a times-table.

'And so it did. Have you thoughts on who might have spoken for you?'

I kept the curiosity I felt from my voice.

'Aye sir, but I don't feel obliged to share my thoughts with a stranger.'

'In that case I will tell you, and you can judge if we are of like mind. Lord Cecil spoke of you as one who had done good service to the Queen.' Relief must have shown in my face. The man leaned closer. 'He spoke well for you, well enough to keep you from gaol, but those who know about such things thought his defence circumspect and wondered if he kept you at liberty because you know so much of his world.' He was very close now and whispering. His breath tickled my cheek. 'The dwarf Cecil keeps you safe, but only so long as you are of use, and that time is running out.'

'Time is always running out.'

'True, but yours need not end so soon.' He leaned back in his chair. 'Another voice was raised in your defence. That of my master. His words carry great sway.'

'I would like the opportunity to thank him.'

'The opportunity may come.' The smile was back. 'Meanwhile be satisfied he has your welfare at heart.'

I chose my words carefully.

'It is always good to have an ally, but difficult to accept aid when ignorant of the source.'

'Surely a man in your position will welcome aid from any quarter?'

'Not without knowing the price.'

The man opened his hands, laying his soft pink palms before me, beginning negotiations with all the craft of a market trader.

'The price is one you can pay while gaining credit and releasing yourself from the difficulties that presently menace you.'

I feigned disinterest.

'I may escape them anyway.'

'My master is a good friend, but he would take it most hard should you refuse to assist him.'

'The difficulty remains. If I do not know your master, I cannot trust his promises or his threats.'

He smiled.

'His threats are promises.'

'Then let him proceed.' I got to my feet. 'I might work for Mephistopheles if I thought the bargain well struck. But I will not attach myself to a man too cowardly to reveal his identity.'

He looked up at me.

'Though the prize be your life?'

I stepped towards the door but something held me within the room. Perhaps it was the hope that he might save me.

'I live yet.'

He spoke with dreadful seriousness.

'None of us know the hour, but few rush towards it.'

'Alliances with absent men won't increase my span. I'm not friendless. I'll take my chances.'

'Aye, and perish.'

'If it be so, it will be so.'

I turned to leave at the same time as a second door at the back of the room opened. The noise made me turn, just as a man I recognised entered.

The absence of the Privy Council did not diminish his authority. My old interrogator was wearing the same austere robes of the previous morning. On his head was a soft hat of black velvet. It gave him the look of a necromancer, though I feel sure that was not his intention. The old man nodded to his deputy, who returned the greeting. Then he turned to me. His voice was mild and stern.

'So you would work for the Devil, Master Marlowe?'

For a second I thought he was about to declare himself Lucifer come to tempt me. I shook my head, half to refute his charge, half at my own folly.

'It was an expression forced from me in an ill-considered moment.'

'Aye, but you are a man for sale.'

'I am a poet.'

'And a spy.' I kept silent, wanting to know what he had to say. 'There has been enough jousting of words in this room. Sit.'

He pointed to the chair I had just vacated and I obeyed, trying not to look too much like a trained dog. He sighed as he eased his old bones into a seat, sandwiching me between the two men. When he turned towards me, the pain of rheumatics distorted his features and I wondered if old age was a goal worth fighting for. He wiped a hand across his face.

'Do poets have many friends?'

'Some.'

'And spies, how many friends can they afford?'

'You ask the wrong man.'

'I would have thought it a question you are ideally suited to answering.' He smiled. 'A spy can't afford any friends. Not one. Even his wife may be in the pay of the enemy.'

'I have no wife.'

'No,' he smiled again, 'you don't. Well then, your closest companion, your patron, even.' I tried to keep my face blank, but perhaps it betrayed my fear, for the old man's eyes widened. 'Yes, no brotherly love in your profession.' He smoothed his beard thoughtfully. 'Not even amongst brothers.'

'What do you want?'

'I want to ease your difficulties.'

'And in return?'

'Bring us Raleigh.'

★

Raleigh changes any room he enters. Sometimes it is as if a window has been opened. Sometimes as if a door has slammed. Soldier, sailor, spy, Raleigh has lived many lives since he left his father's farm. Alchemist, courtier, bard, not so long ago he was the Queen's darling. He still trails a touch of her magic, though he forsook her favour for the love of a lover long past a maid. Adventurer, chronicler, knave. Tall and spare,

Raleigh has the curly hair and rose-gold sheen of the boglanders he ran to ground in Ireland. But he is more muscled than they. His body is a canvas for fine fabric, and you can be sure that when courtier Raleigh bridged a puddle for the Queen, the cloak he forfeited was a fine one.

Raleigh is all style and some substance. His pointed beard has a natural curl that men who spend an early morning hour with a barber and hot tongs can never quite achieve. A large pearl bobs recklessly from his left ear, reminding us of the buccaneer beneath the poet. He is high and low. He can rape and kill, woo and versify. He has thrown bishops from their livings and gilded the way to new worlds. Raleigh is the most calculating of men, and reckless with it.

Raleigh is a fine pirate and a bad spy. He's adept at fiction and poor at deceit. He can weigh smoke. Challenge God. He keeps company with wizards and magi, earls and the Queen's advisors and finds they are the same men. He has dealt in slaughter and massacres. Settled Virginia and lost the new world. He is the conquered man who will write history and so win the last battle, a fine friend and a better enemy.

★

I sat back in my chair and shook my head.

'I have enough enemies without adding Raleigh to the ranks.'

'Raleigh is more general than foot soldier. How do you know he's not marshalling what remains of his powers against you right now?'

'He has no need.'

'He might if rumours suggested you were about to betray him.'

I remembered the old gaoler's advice. His hints of powerful men who might buy my life with theirs. My thoughts had drifted on that tide more than once. But if talk was already circulating of how I might damn Raleigh, I was as good as wrecked. I feigned bravado and said, 'I'm not so desperate I'd conjure the betrayal of a man I hardly know. All that stands against me are vague rumours which, having no substance, will die of their own accord.'

The old man nodded to his assistant, who rose in wordless understanding and retrieved the document he had been signing when I entered. He laid it before me with the assurance of a man revealing a trump card.

There in front of me were all my blasphemies of the night before, black on white, crawling across the page. The clerk who transcribed it had a fine hand. But his twirling capitals and curving curlicues were nothing to my flourishes. The pace of the evening was in my talk. It was a shame it had not been illuminated by the monks of old. They could have punctuated the text with gilded cups of ale. Here one drink sponsoring mild dissension, a second embellishing the theme, a third, fourth, fifth promoting profanities which might hang me. My own words ripped at my body, a stone in my stomach, claw at my throat. The sensation seemed like an augur of the gallows and the quarterman and for the first time in this strange adventure I panicked. I snarled, 'What lies are these?'

And moved to grab the page, but the younger man was quicker. He whisked the paper swift from beneath my reaching fingers. As my palm hit the table the old man moved, faster than I could have guessed, stabbing his knife into the back of my hand, with no more hesitation than if it had been a lump of wood or slice of fruit. He marked his aim, slick-sliding into the difficult channel betwixt the bones, straight through it seemed. I roared and the knife withdrew as fast as it had pierced. The servant who'd first brought me dived into the room. He took in the scene, relaxing as he noted it was my blood and not his master's that pooled the table.

'Marlowe has had an accident, perhaps you could oblige him with a bandage?'

I held my hand against my chest, aware of the blood ruining my doublet, but too seared by pain to let go. The steward returned with hot water and a dressing, which he applied with battlefield expertise. The old man smiled.

'Perhaps I should have mentioned, this is not the only copy of the document. They are signed and witnessed and coupled with the charges already against you . . .'

He trailed off as if too polite to mention the consequences should my blasphemies be revealed. The old man's tone betrayed nothing of the drama between us, but I fancied there was a better colour in his cheeks. 'There is a need for blood. It will either be yours or Raleigh's. Raleigh's would suit me best, but yours will do should circumstance insist.'

I spoke through gritted teeth.

'What is your proposition?'

'If you sign an affidavit against Raleigh we will destroy this document and aid you in your current difficulties.'

'And if not?'

'No one can help a man who will not help himself.'

★

They gave me two days. I clutched my bandaged hand and stared at the scores on the table wondering if they had all been gouged by the old man's knife. His tone was mildness and business now, weighing the cost of my life as a merchant weighs his stock.

'You would be well advised to sign immedi-ately. We would remove Raleigh and with him any threat he may pose to you.'

'I'll take the two days' grace.'

'At the end of that we will send someone to meet with you. You can sign and watch the evidence against you burn, or take the consequences. The choice is yours.'

'Are you Tamburlaine?' I asked, half dazed. And he laughed.

'Put that impostor from your mind. Whoever he might be, his threats are nothing compared to ours.'

'Death is the same whoever brings it.'

He gave me a last look and asked, 'Do you really think so?'

★

That night I followed the Thames out of the city. A full moon lit my progress, hanging low in the sky as if the weight of its silver was dragging it from the firmament. The moon man's face gaped, eyes shocked wide, mouth frozen in a warning scream. Around him stars glowed brilliant as any theatre backcloth. I looked up at the heavens and felt alone. Below me the river pressed on, dark and relentless, swirling with secret currents. I wondered how many deaths it held. Pregnancies and broken hearts, murders slid beneath its tide, drunkards, debtors, kittens and cuckolds all lost. I wondered if the day would ever come when the dead would rise from its embrace and face their persecutors. I repeated to myself the final line of Baynes's note to the Council, 'I think all men in Christianity ought to endeavour that the mouth of so dangerous a member may be stopped.' And vowed that if I were murdered to drag my dead body from whatever grave it were thrown in and hound my foes beyond mercy.

★

Priest Parsons said Raleigh ran a school for atheists, where men learned to spell God backwards.

But I doubt Raleigh would entertain any incapable of that poor trick. All of one summer I was a frequent visitor to Sherborne, the palace the Queen had plucked from a bishop's living when she was Raleigh's Cynthia. There was no conjuring done there. But Raleigh was host to amazing men. When he swapped one Bess for another and so lost influence, things that had only been whispered against him began to be said out loud.

Men like me were poison to Raleigh's reputation. But he thought us worth the risk. It was at his house that I met Thomas Harriot, who had ventured to the new world. Harriot told us that these new lands were awash with antiquities, which preceded Moses's time and that the natives there had histories of their own which recorded no great flood. Under Raleigh's roof we questioned the composition of souls, smoked tobacco and got drunk on dangerous talk.

Though it would grieve me, I was willing to betray Raleigh to save myself. But Raleigh's star had risen and fallen so many times, I wasn't sure that to be the agent of his demise would secure my life. Yet rumours that I was out to dispose of him would certainly be a death penalty. Men do not live as long and as close to the sun as Raleigh has without being ruthless enough to dispatch rivals, however much he might like their verse. After all, poetry can be pressed between the pages of other works while the poet's head grins on a spike or lolls in a ditch.

I wasn't reckless in my preparations. I'd disguised myself as best I could, tying my hair back and dressing in working men's clothes. It was not the first time I had worn this guise and I liked myself well enough in the simple cloth breeches and waistcoat. But it seemed, as I'd watched my reflection shave by candlelight, that I was no longer the handsome dramatist who had beguiled Walsingham a few short days ago. There were lines where there had been none before. And it struck me that if this adventure saw my death, I would not die a young man.

★

Mortlake, there's a dread about that name. The village has no pond, but I fancy there must have been one once. Some stagnant tarn so wreathed in mist and bloated with bodies that the villagers filled it in, though they could not banish its name. I'd muffled my horse's shoes with sacking, but the dull thud of his hooves sounded loud against the deathly quiet of the hamlet. No lights shone from windows, no dogs barked at my approach. All were abed, tucked safe and warm between the sheets, and it was eerie to be the only man moving in that deserted place. I guided my horse along the main street, turned towards the church and saw, frozen on the opposite side of the road, a dark-robed figure standing tall and slender in the moonlight.

Despite the losses he had suffered since we'd last met, his sixty years sat easy on Dr Dee. The old magus opened his garden gate, making no comment on my disguise, and invited me through with an abstracted air I knew belied the sharpness of his wit. The geography of Dee's home is hard to fathom. Under the doctor's hand his mother's simple dwelling has sprouted long winding corridors which wrap around and through themselves, budding new rooms, branching into halls, encrusting the old house in a labyrinth where somewhere hides his library, laboratories and secret oratories. The house was wreathed in smells as complex as its map. I thought I could detect sulphur and dung in the mix and decided to analyse no more. Dee's sure step led on and I followed, wishing I had a trail of pebbles or ball of string to aid my return. He spoke a little as we walked, glancing back over his shoulder to cast reassuring smiles laced with pity. His Celtic lilt gave a freshness to his speech. But they were inconsequential words, designed to put me at my ease and I replied in dull fashion. Soon he fell silent and the only sound was the fall of our footsteps and the soft sweeping of Dee's robe. Eventually, when we were somewhere near the centre of the house, he led me into a small octagonal room lined with books and bade me sit. He busied himself at a stove and I wondered what kind of necromancy he was engaged on. When he joined me at the table he passed me an herbal tincture. I smelled it, then took a sip. The liquid was warm and bland. Dee sensed my hesitation.

'Nothing intoxicating or entrancing, just a mix of peppermint and other herbs good for digestion.'

'You think my stomach out of sorts?'

The doctor's beard descended half his chest, seeming soft and white as swansdown against his dark artist's robe. He smiled tiredly. Lines of age and hardship, which had seemed absent before, revealed themselves. He took a sip of his own draft.

'It does no harm and might do good.'

I nodded and took another drink, though it tasted so filthy I thought only intoxication could excuse it. We sat in silence. In the next room a row of stills bubbled mysteriously.

'Do your researches go well?' I asked.

He lowered his eyes.

'They near their end.'

His meaning came to me and I marvelled at the ease in his voice. But then Dee is somewhere over sixty and I am not yet thirty. Perhaps it was no wonder my tone was not so sure.

'I fear my days may also be nearing their end. There are plots against me.' I hesitated, drawing my hand across my brow, massaging my temples. Dee nodded at me to go on. 'I've been asked to hand Raleigh to a faction of the Council in return for documents which incriminate me.' The old man nodded again. His calmness irritated me and I snapped, 'You don't seem surprised.'

'Why should it be surprising when men who deal in danger and then seek out more jeopardy find themselves the agents of each other's doom? Raleigh has already been here on the same business.'

I felt regret and relief that our paths hadn't crossed.

'What did you decide?' I asked.

Dee spoke softly.

'Whatever influence I had is as diminished as my fortunes. We are entering a new age and all I can offer is guidance. I advised Raleigh as I will advise you. Make a pact through me.'

'Easy counsel, I've no desire for Raleigh's blood but if the choice is his or mine, I won't hesitate.'

'He said the same.'

'Then we are at odds. If I don't hand Raleigh over, I die.'

Dee smiled sadly.

'If you try, even if you succeed, you'll die. Raleigh will make certain of it.'

'So I die either way?'

'All I can say is Raleigh will not countenance any attack from you. Sign papers against him, and you sign your own death warrant. Undertake to leave him alone and should you die, he'll grant you immortality.'

I looked around the room taking in Dee's jars and books, the potions and strange instruments that aid him in his famous art. I laughed.

'Old man, I do not wish to be immortal as a speck of dust or wisp of smoke, nor do I wish to become one of your angels.' I smiled. 'I doubt the gown would fit.'

Dee shook his head impatiently.

'Your ignorance shines like phosphor. How could I make you immortal? I said *he* offers you immortality – Raleigh. He wants an alliance. If you promise not to sign this affidavit, he pledges not to dispatch you. He can't banish your enemies, but he reveres your talent. Raleigh promises not to pursue you if you make a pact. He also undertakes that should you die, he'll ensure your writings live beyond your death, beyond these troubled times and into the future.'

'Raleigh makes a promise he can't deliver. My work will die with me.'

'No. For a while it may seem lost, but there are always men who recognise worth. We will keep your flame alive with them and when the time is right sow the seeds of your renaissance. I guarantee that if you spare Raleigh, even if it be your death, men will know of the genius of Christopher Marlowe. Four hundred years hence and beyond they will perform your plays and write your story. Surely,' Dee smiled kindly, 'that is the only immortality you would acknowledge?'

★

Night was fading by the time I left Dee, but the river looked no better by dawn's light. I wondered what kind of a death drowning would be, thought of Raleigh and remembered his talk of voyages to the New World.

One evening when pipe smoke had mellowed our talk from science into reminiscence, he'd told me how the green bloated body of a stranger had once rushed from the deep, fallen from some other vessel he supposed, though he had thought his ship the only one to reach these uncharted waters. The body had bobbed on the surf, riding the tide as round and as buoyant as an inflated bladder. The captain had ordered the crew to drown the cursed man again. But sailors are superstitious, they'd claimed it an augur of the future and defied him to the point of mutiny. The captain had retreated and the drowned man trailed them half a day, caught in the ship's swell, banging against the hull with the even thud of an undertaker's hammer until they lost him somewhere in the terror-stricken night.

★

I'd asked Dee if he had any knowledge of Tamburlaine. He'd stared into the distance.

'If Kelly were here, he could skry for us. I've no doubt he might find the identity of your foe in the crystals.'

I'd shaken my head.

'I trust your wisdom more than his. I've told you all I know, what does it make you think?'

'This person tries to write in your fashion? The style of the note was yours you say?'

'Inferior to mine, but with the same rhythm, he talked of my plays.'

Dee had smiled.

'You're vain even *in extremis*.'

Then he'd laid his hands on the table and raised his face upwards. Dee's mouth took on a serious set and his eyes lost their focus. The candles flickered. Shadows hung in the hollows of his face, and I felt I could see the skull beneath the skin as white as any death mask. We sat for a moment in silence, then he began to speak in his soft voice, his Welsh accent more pronounced than before, hesitating now and then as he grasped for words.

'The person who wrote this libel admires you even as he sets in motion wheels that may kill you . . . He cloaks himself in the identity of your creation, as near to being you as he can get . . . He would rather make himself Marlowe, but while Marlowe lives he will settle on the most ruthless of your heroes. Or perhaps the one he thinks most like you . . . There is jealousy and love in this mix. Your enemy Tamburlaine is a man who wishes to be you and yet wishes to kill you . . . and so invites his own death.'

'Tell me his name,' I'd commanded.

Dee had started from his trance, alert and rested.

'How can I?' His tone was sharp. 'Only you and he can know who Tamburlaine is.'

And all at once I realised I might.

★

Blind Grizzle's was dark, veiled in shadow and as silent as the charnel chapel. I called his name as I entered, expecting Hector's growl to echo my greeting, but the only sound was a soft tinkling from the bells that strung the ceiling. I wandered through the bookshelves, past the old man's empty chair, trying not to trip on any of his booby traps, drawing my sword against the dark and the silence, though it pained my injured hand. I hesitated at the door to Grizzle's private quarter, then swiftly pushed it wide.

The interrogator had been right. Death wasn't the same whoever brought it. Hector was splayed across the floor. Dispatched by a swift cut to the throat. His fate had been better than his master's. The old man lay drowned in his own blood, draped across the bed Blaize and I had sat on two days before. The killer had played with Grizzle. The tracks of a sharp blade descended like bloody tears down each of the old man's cheeks. His mouth had been slit wide into a harlequin smile and his cheekbones bloodied by a crosshatch of cuts until they resembled the rouged cheeks of a player. It struck me the mutilation had been torture designed to find his fabled fortune. The injustice of the old man's death, killed for a rumour of gold, hit me and I lashed out with my good hand, pushing a bookcase to the floor.

The bookseller's cloudy eyes were wide open in death. He'd told me once he could see the difference between light and dark. Now everything was black. I dropped down on my haunches, leaning forward to close his eyes, hoping but doubting he'd died before mutilation began. I've seen many dead men, but most died knowing the risks. I swore that if I ever found Grizzle's killer, I'd become the agent of his long and painful death. Hector's eyes were open too, dark brown shot back into his skull. I didn't bother to close them but found myself stroking a finger along the rough hair of his nose. A touch he would never have tolerated from me when he was alive.

If I hadn't bent to give those last simple ministrations I would have missed it, the envelope was so steeped in blood. It lay there tossed on the corpse of my old acquaintance. Even if it hadn't borne my name in the same cursive hand as the other messages, I would have known it was intended for me. I tore the seal, sure of what lay within, a scrap of linen as black as Grizzle's future. But where my other missives had been blank this held one word, white chalked across it, *SOON*. I hesitated. The horrible suspicion that had sprouted tentative roots in my mind was coming into full flower. Then all thought was banished by sounds from the front-shop.

Whether it was the noise of my rage or Hector's silence that had alerted the stallholders I didn't know. But three low voices were heading my way. I realised how I must appear, a desperate bloodstained character, standing sword drawn over a corpse. The back room was windowless and tiny, piled high with books. The only furniture was the simple pallet of a bed, which bore the old man. There was nowhere to hide so I kept my sword by my side, took a deep breath and secreted myself behind the door.

I peered through the slit in the doorjamb. For a full second the horror of the corpses held the men. They fell silent, looking at the blood-painted face of their friend. Then, as if a spell had lifted, everyone moved at once. One ran to raise the alarm, while the other two dropped to their knees, checking for signs of life, though they must have known him dead. The men's low whispers mingled prayers and expletives. They glanced at each other, like hostages in a dream realm. I knew this daze would pass, shock would turn to anger and my inevitable discovery would be fatal. The only hope lay in escape.

I slid beyond the door and landed a hard boot in the centre of each of their rears, knocking them off balance and onto the bloody bodies of Grizzle and Hector. I didn't like the further desecration of the old man's corpse, or that of his dog, but I had no urge to catch their condition. The muffled shouts of the felled booksellers followed me, but I didn't look back as I ran, hurdling the booby-trapped piles of books, ripping the strings of bells that tangled my hair, praying no one would enter before I had fled. I thanked the Fates Grizzle's shop was in the loneliest portion of the churchyard and ran towards the chapel, hiding myself amongst the long grass that edged the graves, peeling off my bloodied jerkin. Hoping my white shirt had escaped the stain of blood.

★

Dee had been firm in his insistence that only I could know the identity of Tamburlaine. I'd said, 'So I'm to give you my life and you give me nothing?'

'You may escape your other enemies and Raleigh offers you a considerable thing, the survival of your work. How many great works have died with their author? Of your plays only *Tamburlaine* is printed in ink.'

'My patron may do that anyway.'

Dee had looked away.

'What?'

His answer, when it came, was hesitant.

'Your patron is a weak man. He loves you, but finds Raleigh and the Council more persuasive. He stands between the two and does nothing.'

'And so he knows of this?'
'Walsingham knows many things.'

★

Walsingham and I had been alone and drunk often, with nothing but fellow feeling between us. Now I wondered if he had bedded me because he knew it was the last time we would be together. Maybe he felt a rush of affection for his old protégé. Maybe he thought dead men don't tell tales. I wondered if he felt my flesh grow cold beneath his touch, if he had smelled decay on the mouth he left unkissed. I wondered if he saw the glow pleasure cast on my face and imagined these drained lips peeled back against my teeth, the cheeks and brow he caressed specked green with rot. I shivered. My patron had surpassed any vice of mine. He had slept with a dead man.

I thought of all of this as I lay in the high, damp grass of the churchyard, listening for the sound of pursuers. Tiny insects plied their trades, bustling to and fro like costermongers setting up stall on market day. The smell of earth and meadows reminded me of childhood and I remembered listening to my brothers' calls as they searched for me one long hot afternoon. I'd watched them from my hiding place, refusing to be found, relishing the power concealment brought. It was a long time since I'd thought of those days and the remembrance added to my unease, for surely every man remembers his beginnings when he is about to die.

★

Eventually, when it seemed a long time since I had heard the crash of pursuers, I slipped from my hiding place and made for the embankment. My mind swam; Dee's voice echoed in my head and I felt the ghosts of Grizzle and Hector join me, running at my side through the streets. I welcomed them with a shout and they whispered the name of my enemy soft in my ear. They seemed happy with their role in this poor play without encores. Tamburlaine had set the first act and led me through his shadow show, but the death of the old man and his dog were a new beginning, an overture to slaughter. I would rewrite history. This time, Tamburlaine must die.

★

Blaize cut a ridiculous figure. My tall and hirsute friend strode across the stage decked in a woman's gown several sizes too small. It gaped at the back where the stays refused to meet. The bodice rode high on his waist, the lace-trimmed neckline stretched across his chest just low enough to reveal a thicket of hair. He was instructing a group of apprentice players on how to act like a lady. Though the objective eye would never cast Blaize in a female role, he made a fine matron. There was no mincing in his walk, hardly any sway at all in fact, just the sensation of soft round hips gliding beneath the skirt. The apprentices watched him spellbound. It should have been a scene to warm the heart of any playwright, but I was already on fire with fury. I charged through the empty audience pit roaring like a baited bear. Blaize heard me and turned. His face lit up, then just as quick his smile was extinguished. He made a bow, whose flourishes were all mockery, and drew himself upright, salting my savaged heart with Kyd's words.

> *Awake Revenge, if love, as love hath had,*
> *Have yet the power or prevalence in hell.*

Icarus's wings could not have hastened my approach. I charged onto the stage, drawing my sword in my injured hand, fury beating the pain from me. The apprentices scattered to the sidelines. I must have made a terrible figure. My hair was tangled with grass and twigs. A day's growth disfigured my face, the bandages that wrapped my pierced hand were grass-stained and bloody, and the wound Baynes had inflicted in my side had leaked onto my shirt.

Theatre would demand we parlayed for a while. Set out our dispute in fine phrases before embarking on the brawl. Blaize saw me coming

and ran. But ladies' gowns are not designed for
flight. I caught the tail of his skirt, upended him
and kicked him on the jaw. Something snapped
and he howled, tooth, blood and spit spraying
the stage. The tide of little boys surged backwards. One began to cry, but most were actor
enough to close observe our fray. Blaize tried to
rise. I kicked him on the head and he fell forward,
crawling away from me on all fours, his dress
trailing a red smear of blood. I let him creep across
half the stage, then strode to where he tried to
rise and stood hard on his hand, feeling bones
give beneath my foot, then pulled him upright
by the same ruined limb. The apprentices' worried
jabber reached me over Blaize's pleas and groans.

'Watch boys, and learn,' I shouted. 'This is
the theatre of blood.'

It seemed the funniest thing in the world and
I started to laugh as I pitched my old companion
downwards with a punch to his broken jaw and a
kick in the ribs.

Two stage-hands edged from the wings. I
drew my sword.

'My quarrel is with Judas here, but come forward if you want some of this.' I brandished the blade. 'There's enough for him and extra for you if you want it.'

The men hesitated, then retreated back from whence they came. But I knew it wouldn't be long before they returned with help. One of the boys ran towards his master.

'Keep away from him,' I growled, grasping him under the arms and hurling him into a crowd of his fellows. 'Unless you want to feel the sharp end of my sword!'

Blaize pulled himself half upright. He leaned, dazed and damaged against a pillar, holding his injured jaw. He looked up at the painted heavens that tent the stage, as if searching for some sign. Then shook his head softly in wonder and turned to face me. His eyes, deep and innocent, stared heartbroken into mine. He slurred through spit and blood.

'What fury is this? Have you lost your senses?'

I put my sword to his face, scoring two deep

rents down his cheeks, marking him as he had marked the old man.

'Familiar? No doubt you meant me take the blame for that death too?'

He shook his head and his voice returned weak and defeated.

'I love you.'

'Like the Devil loves holy water.'

'No, like a brother.'

'Then let us decide now who is Cain and who Abel.' I laughed bitterly. 'We'll rewrite history and the ablest of us will live.'

'You have crippled me.'

'And you have killed me.'

I became aware of a bustle down in the audience pit.

'Our business isn't finished.'

I dragged Blaize to his feet and huckled him into the labyrinth of dark corridors that lead from the stage to the recesses of the theatre and up towards the gods.

★

I pushed Blaize ahead of me. His blood spotted the steps, leaving a trail for our pursuers.

'Stop bleeding,' I barked.

And he made a bitter noise that might have been a laugh. We were in a dark corridor, dusty with disuse. I shoved him onwards, towards a dim flight of stairs. No one had been here since the start of the Plague and cobwebs strung the stairwell. As we climbed I wondered how many of the playgoers who had busied these passages with anticipation now lay in Plague pits. I remembered how the noise of the audience stretched into the tiring house, adding an edge to the actors' preparations. How we would hold each other's gaze and bet on the size of the crowd, guessing their mass by the measure of their roar. And suddenly the memory was so real I had to stop, sure it must be the noise of a chase behind us. But all was graveyard quiet and we resumed our climb, Blaize's low groans the only sound. At last we reached a turning in the lobby, the kind of dark place where women are assaulted for their honour and their jewellery. I pushed him up against the damp wall, stuck a knife at his throat and spat one word into his face.

'Why?'

For a second I thought he was going to deny everything, perhaps I hoped he would, for when he raised his head and I saw tears glistering his eyelashes, my fractured world shattered. I whispered, 'Oh you really did it. You killed me. You're talking to a dead man, dead man.'

It was hard to believe this was the Thomas Blaize who had held whole audiences in his sway. He clutched his hand to his broken jaw and his voice was tired and muffled with pain.

'I never meant it to end this way.'

Frustration made me shake him. Blaize kept his hand at his chin, but offered no resistance, letting the back of his head bang against the wall until I stopped for fear I'd dash his brains from their skull.

'You owe me names.' I slammed his head again for emphasis. 'You haven't the guile to achieve all this on your own. Tell me who stands behind you and I'll grant you a few more last breaths.'

Blaize looked into my eyes.

'We were the best of friends.'

I hit him again, knocking his hand from his face. A thin stream of blood flew from his mouth splattering the wall like a devilish signature. He staggered and I caught him.

'Now talk.'

Blaize placed his hand back on his wounded face as if its presence lifted some of the pain. His voice was broken and at times he faltered. But there were no more appeals to friendship or times past. He turned inwards, searching for the truth of the story as he told it.

'It's hard to light upon beginnings. Months ago, when the theatres first closed, I found myself in difficulties.'

He hesitated.

'What kind of difficulties?'

'The usual kind. Some men came to my assistance.'

'They lent you money?' Blaize nodded. 'For love?'

He laughed.

'The days when my love could bring an income are long past. No, I was to make their investment grow, though I needed it to live. When the time came to repay, I found myself without even the principal.'

'And no plan?'

'I thought perhaps the old man,' he wiped his face. 'I thought perhaps he would help. The sum he advanced was too small.'

'So you killed him?'

'No! Yes.' He shook his head. 'Not straight away. This all happened months ago, before you departed for Walsingham's.'

'So even then there were plots against me?'

His sigh hung in the air.

'I met them to ask for time. I knew that as soon as the Plague lifted I would have a means to make money. But they gave me a beating, threatened my life, then offered me a way out.'

'Your life for mine.'

'It wasn't so simple. They represented powerful men. They told me that if I thought of a way to bring you before the Council then these men would free me of my debt.' Blaize's voice grew querulous. 'You'd abandoned me to the Plague and the city. I did as they asked to save my skin, trusting you to shake yourself free. You have before.'

I shook my head in wonder. He had killed Kyd, Grizzle and me, for a bag of gold.

'I would have given you money.'

'Money and contempt.'

There was a loathing in his voice I hadn't heard before. A realisation dawned.

'It wasn't just the money,' I whispered. 'You wrote those notes. I knew you jealous but I never guessed the depths of your envy. You hate me.'

Blaize shook his head.

'You took my love and warped it. Laughed at my literary works. Introduced me as *one of* the finest actors in London, never *the* finest. Played tricks on me. Made me step through Hell's mouth then gave the magician's role to another, leaving me to play the servant once again. You cast me in the role of murderer and so I became one.' He dropped his head. 'But hate has fled now that we're equals.'

I looked at his blood-spattered form hunched against the wall and laughed.

'Some Faustian King you'd make. You're a half-rate actor and a no-rate poet. A scurvy cove who kills old men for effect. You leave your little notes to add more theatre to the chase, but also because you needed me to find you. To be your audience, admire you in the role of killer, when all the time you're just the hired helper of a hired hand. I'll kill you with as much regret as I'd kill an insect. You've never been my equal, never will be.'

A spasm crossed Blaize's face, but he managed to grin through it.

'The dead are equal.'

I leaned in close, scored another cut across his face and hissed, 'The dead are dead.'

Blaize shuddered in pain, then forced a laugh.

'You always had a way with words. So you mean to kill me?'

'Do you doubt it?'

'No.' My lost friend shook his head. 'You and I have reached our final act.'

'My final act will be to kill you.'

He leered, his grin shining wolfishly in the dark. It was a look I'd loved and I struck out once more with my sword hoping to slash it from his face. Blaize screamed and put his hand to the flap of flesh hanging from his cheek. He whispered, 'One last kiss and I'll save you a task, dead man.'

And shoved his bloodied self against me, his lips scraping my brow. I slammed him into the wall and Blaize's wild laughter rang through the deserted hallway.

'Now, or I'll do it for you.'

I watched as he unfastened the bodice, dropping the dress to the floor, standing before me in only his britches, exposing the chest I had lain on, the dark hair that tangled across his breast, then trailed like an arrow to his navel and below. Desire caught me unawares. My fingers tingled with the anticipation of touch. But the thought of Kyd and Grizzle stayed me. I watched as Blaize pulled out his dagger and turned its cut-throat blade upon himself. Looked on as he winced at its contact, not in pain but at the iciness of the metal against skin that would soon feel nothing. He hesitated.

'We travelled far together. Will you hold my hand at the start of this journey?'

And I spat on him.

'Even if we meet in Hell I'll damn you.'

A tear leaked down his cheek. He wiped it away and pressed the knife further, wincing. He saw how it must be done and turned to face the wall, preparing to dash himself against it and fall on his blade, Roman style. I looked away. Heard Blaize take a deep breath, that blew into a warrior yell, then felt a rush of air as his body charged towards me and he turned, knife in hand, lunging at my throat. But I had known him long times and had my own blade waiting. I ducked his move, then caught him close, sticking my knife deep into his belly. His eyes rolled back to meet my gaze.

'You were never Tamburlaine,' I told him,

'just a half-rate actor. No match for fear or fatal steel.'

I held Blaize to me for what seemed like an age, feeling his gasps fade into sighs, twisting the dagger slowly, until I realised the heat of his breath was gone and let the body crumple to the ground, softening his descent though I knew he could feel no more pain. My comrade lay broken at my feet, his face a bloody mess, but his eyes the same deep brown I'd loved. I turned my back and walked away, scraping my sword down the wall of the staircase in a rattle that couldn't drown the silence.

★

Last night I received a summons to a house in Deptford. There I will be held to accounts, which cannot be squared. Life is frail and I may die today. But Tamburlaine knows no fear. My candles are done, the sky glows red and it looks as if the day is drenched in blood. I finish this account and prepare for battle in the sureness that life is the only prize worth having and the knowledge that there are worse fates than damnation. If these are the last words I write, let them be,

A Curse on Man and God.

Christopher Marlowe
30th May 1593

Christopher Marlowe was knifed to death at a house in Deptford, on the evening of Wednesday 30th May, 1593.

AUTHOR'S NOTE

*T*he death of Christopher Marlowe is a mystery
which will never be solved. History has be-
queathed us a tantalising framework of facts – the
Elizabethans were as prolific as the Stasi when it came
to official documents. Yet the facts can't tell us the
full tale and historians' theories on Marlowe's death
are ultimately well informed, meticulously researched
speculation.

The debate is not confined to historians.
Type *Christopher Marlowe Death* into any Internet
search engine and you'll raise thousands of
websites and chat rooms devoted to the poet's
demise. American coroners debate the nature of
his wounds, conspiracy theorists think his death
a ruse designed to cover escape and believe
Marlowe the author of Shakespeare's better
plays. It's cheering that a mystery, which was a

source of conjecture and rumours in the 1590s, still exercises so many 21st-century minds.

Thomas Beard in his *Theatre of God's Judgement* (1597), a series of obituaries relishing God's revenge on wayward individuals, has no doubt that Marlowe's atheism was the cause of his untimely end. Beard alleges that Marlowe's hand was grabbed by his opponent in a knife fight, and the blade forced into the poet's own eye. A scenario that pleases Beard no end.

> '. . . hee compelled his own hand which had written those blasphemies to be the instrument to punish him, and that in his brain which had devised the same . . . hee euen cursed and blasphemed to his last gaspe, and togither with his breath an oth flew out his mouth . . .'[1]

Another theory is that a serving man, a rival of

[1] Quoted in The Nonesuch Press, Hotson, J. Leslie and G. L. Kittredge, *Death of Christopher Marlowe*, p.11 (1925)

Marlowe's 'in his lewde loue', administered the blow.[2]

According to the official inquest, Christopher Marlowe, Ingram Frizer, Robert Poley and Nicholas Skeres were companions in a day-long drinking and feasting session which was reaching its close by six that evening. Witness accounts have Marlowe reclining on a bed. The other three still at table, Frizer sandwiched himself between Poley and Skeres with his back towards Marlowe. The poet and Frizer began arguing about who was to pay the bill. Marlowe, suffused by anger at some statement of Frizer's, leapt from the bed, grabbing a knife from his opponent's belt, attacking and wounding him in the head. Frizer, wedged between the two other men and in fear of his life, struggled with Marlowe, eventually managing to gain control of the knife, and struck Marlowe a mortal wound over his right eye, penetrating his brain and killing him instantly.

The coroner's jury accepted the killer's

[2] Meres, Frances, *Palladis Tamia* (1598), Ibid.

claims of self-defence, supported by witnesses Poley and Skeres, the evidence of his own superficial head wounds, and the fact that he didn't abscond. So Marlowe's killer was awarded a pardon.

The flaws in the jury's decision have been well established, notably by Charles Nicholl.[3] Ingram Frizer, Robert Poley and Nicholas Skeres are variously con men, extortioners, double agents, fences and international spies. They have connections with the murkier fringes of Elizabethan politics, are well known to Marlowe's patron, and factions of the Privy Council and the underworld of more than one city. The keeper of Marshalsea prison said of Poley: 'He will beguile you of your wife or of your life.'[4] The official account rests on the unreliable testimony of three rogues and is therefore unsafe. We know that Marlowe died at a house in Deptford. We know the date of his death and the three men present.

[3] Quoted in Nicholl, Charles, *The Reckoning: The Murder of Christopher Marlowe*, Vintage, 2002.
[4] Ibid.

We know the nature of the wound that killed him. Everything else is educated guesswork, or in this author's case, a fiction.

ACKNOWLEDGEMENTS

The responsibility for any inaccuracies within this text lies entirely with me. There are, however, several sources whose help should be acknowledged. Invaluable histories included Charles Nicholl's *The Reckoning* (Vintage, 2002), Peter Blayney's *The Bookshops in Paul's Cross Church-yard* (Bibliographical Society of America, 1990) and Leslie Hotson's *Death of Christopher Marlowe* (The Nonesuch Press, 1925). The inspiration for a novella starring Christopher Marlowe came from a commission by Jamie Byng of Canongate Books. The National Library of Scotland's Robert Louis Stevenson Award and the Hôtel Chevillon in Grez-sur-Loing gave me valuable peace and space in which to begin this narative. My agent David Miller, editor Judy Moir and the novelists Graeme Williamson and Zoë Strachan were each a source of support, advice and suggestions, the best of

which I probably ignored, but would have been
lost without.

Louise Welsh

(2004)